Do You Hear What I Hear

jusTemple

authorHOUSE®

AuthorHouse™
1663 Liberty Drive
Bloomington, IN 47403
www.authorhouse.com
Phone: 1-800-839-8640

Published by AuthorHouse 2/27/2012

ISBN: 978-1-4685-5276-8 (sc)
ISBN: 978-1-4685-5277-5 (hc)
ISBN: 978-1-4685-5278-2 (e)

Library of Congress Control Number: 2012903041

Art work by: Chris M. Elliott
contact: reigndropsinternatioanl@gmail.com

To my children & grandchild
GOD's many blessings and precious gifts

Eldest, Neshia and her son, my grandson Jacob "Lee"
Keyat the middle daughter
Rodney II my only son
& Rodteshia aka Tee Tee my baby

A mother's love should never be under estimate.

Contents

OVERTURE

The time to have an audition with seeing, transforming an investigation within the hearing.

The tale of contrast within a waterfall, as it interviews within the hollow echoes, blinding laughter, and contagious thunders.

Come; come, to connect with Gershom to a level of what's going on with the reflection in the mirror. The signature of the dragon eyes, recap the memoir of the infuriated shark, and a hissing snake in the mist of the switch controller. The signs point to shore, a mass of liquid confusion; enhances a mystery of harsh imprisonment within the agriculture of a tree.

Lights On!

Gershom trail of me, myself, and I, a testing of the sands of times. The strange occurrences are not to be deceived as a lie, because so much truth is right before your eyes. Catch it with your eyes or ears; otherwise you'll have a reversal of mind betrayal.

The exit is a reality of horrifying way to prove, you can't run nor hide. The control of Gershom is with in her means. The test is do you hear what she hears?

Italy 1972

Biography

I'm going on forty years old and also a grandmother, found strives into telling this story, of surviving the game in the truth and a lie, the regeneration of a suspenseful horror.

I'm going to skip pass unrelated details and explain why.

My writing started as a release of my dormant pain "Can you see what I see", and this being the second book its focus is on my sins with exaggeration. The show of how spine-tingling sins can be in a mixture of the ways of the world. In this fictional form of literature, telling my story without forfeiting my emotions. The livelihood of individuality, within the only me there is. I had to set aside the numbing feeling of you can't teach an old dog new tricks. With the expression of you're never too old to learn, hitting my thoughts in an explosion.

My journey maybe a little rough, but as any road or mountain in my path, I must keep going, the strategy of conquering, even in last place. I'm the winner of not quitting, even in the mist of plagues full of rumors that I'm losing, my teachings of do your best.

My bio was intended for you to get to know me, within my works. The work shows, I have a goal. The plan is three and this is jus the second. Future not yet completed.

The rapture within this goal is to get to a spot where I can help, my way with no boundaries. My mirage of existence to others of these goals, created the phantasm name jusTemple. In presentation to a recourse of the plan, release, release, and release with a shocking appeal.

The situation of the plan is to step in with a new wave, putting a dip in my swag. I begin to turn the key of motivation to unlocking a channel of seeing, hearing, and speaking, a gift, full of power.

So understanding of, "Do you hear what I hear," is booming in your ear.

The blast of my weird release with delight in writing, to be heard by the world! I send out much applause to you for flipping chapter to chapter, and amalgamating with the main character. The ending, I will give you a standing ovation.

The force of an insight, that GOD is my strength.

CHAPTER 1

Wonderland Of Horror

Strong male voice, cloudy as it spoke, "Dear John, questioning signs of the times and wonders of miracles."

A shadow on the wall in front of me, darkness was the rest of the surroundings.

The hands of the shadow moving rapidly, "Can forty eight go into four?"

The hands stop, and I started looking towards the source of light.

As I looked up a bright light enter into my pupils, causing a-

Lights off

Lights on

Blinking, a bright flash of light, the eyes open to straight sun. A beam of ray eating at the wet coat of gloss on my eyes, a time for pain to be embrace; a torture of distinguishing, what, within the mind.

Turning my head away from the light was no help.

A sound started to fill my ears, of washing away like a row away paddle moving in the distance of a waterfall.

Lights off

Had to replenish my eyes for moister, this closing was the start of an end.

I slightly begin to feel an improper grip above my knees. Which cause an instant…

Lights ON

Splashing enters my drums, sound waves chattering in the mist. I jumped to my feet, my face facing downwards, waist deep in water, an aqua wall in the mist of my eyes. The grip still in place, I knew if I pulled back, I would fall.

Floating a teal candle, with little fuel, underneath a long shadow moving closer surrounded by cluster of waves, in this deep blue black sea.

Segregation to my ears of rain drops hitting this pool of disclaimed water. Drops creatively forming sounds, the vibration of veins popping within my hand. A fallen of dysfunction with sorcery to the control of the mind.

Hyperthermia, getting swallow by the roots of my hair, digestion of chills.

An unseen hold on the skin causing typhoon to the nerves. I was picking up the sound of small children within nature, moving all about. The direction and travel, I wasn't in comprehension of, the footsteps announced this was their playground.

The exploring and wondering in all spaces, my pigmentation became cold as ice.

The cold removing the feeling of skin, a sensation below the waist and dropping, a supply of circulation to the waist, being shut down.

My hands right above this blueberry tunnel of water, with a Texas tea shadow coming in.

My hands in a workout, the feeling of a grip locking of intertwining fingers. The thumbs last but not least.

A numbness slapping the brain, reaction to the response kept a hold of my body. Frozen in fright, but another emotion getting ready for the stand.

Lights off

Lights on

The wax of the candle, shifted in position. On its last flicker, the flame hanging on to the string.

Shock introduced in small trembles to the water. I couldn't move away as this dark shadow moved closer to me, underneath the water.

One cell still open, I had to find a way out of this darkness at sea. My neck started to tic, a movement of small jerks, head moving upwards, darkness.

Donkeys giggling overwhelming the ear drums, a chamber of enclosing sound. Tempted by the notion of quitting, filled the lungs.

Lights off

A collapse and I was underwater, the temperature put me back on my feet, quick. It release from my calves, of a grip that was disturbing.

Lights on

The teal candle, engulf with water. My eyes ready as I sprung out of the water to my surprise, a red light blinking. The light a shadow from underneath the water, a pool length away, a couple of strokes would get me closer.

Darkness was behind me, I knew it was time to make it to the light.

My eyes journey around my area, the light source changed the coloring of the sea, to dark black red. A ghostly sea of existences, lonely for excitement.

Eyes moving to the dark shadow covering my thighs, underneath getting closer; again. The shadow making viewing of my feet out the question,

Shadowy claws! I felt a tug at my waist.

I felt myself flying in air, jus a touch. Paralyzing my presumption, a channel of hidden waves pushing threw.

Waves of ice cold fright.

A challenge started to occur, a release from the grasp of the claw. I started to shake, as green glowing eyes caught my focus, its peering eyes right above my hands. The shape of this creature was a black blur underwater but the eye color wasn't.

Hyperthermia wasn't the cause of the shakes and jerks, but hysteria was.

Falling back, as it let go of my kicking limbs.

Lights off

Sppllasshhh

Lights on

My head coming out the water, racing to the light source, my feet pushing off the monster shell.

Electricity came in the breathing tube, tingling to my toes and rescuing my lungs. A traffic of major pursuit of survival, adrenaline rush, burst of new energy.

The evolving of survival.

My body gave off a doggie paddle, the light was getting brighter but the shadow was getting closer. My eyes chanted as I stayed a float.

The howl of wolves in my ears, chatting in the darkness. Echoes of surround sounds, my toes felt a strange tug.

Lights off

My mouth reaching the surface first, gasping for air.

Lights on

The redness in the water got brighter. Shadow still underneath, as I made my way to the light as the monster toyed with its entertainment.

My nerves shattering in the mist of a cool sensation, my breathing wrestling for gulps. The fight for freedom of fresh air. I begin to breathe in frozen H2O, with chilling smoothies to my tongue. The icy wetness to my lips was tightening to cracks within the folds, from one cheek to the other. Front teeth slamming up and down on bottom row, as the jocks slither sideways.

Freezer burn to my eyes, corroding my area of focus. Danger of preserving rottenness was coming into play, taking the feeling from my toes first.

Lights off

I'm swimming in hysteria, control was in need.

Lights on

A warm bubble hit my heel, face coming out the water with rage; this is not my destiny of death, not. This comfort to the heel encouraged electric shock to the brain waves.

Wild packs hollering at the sounds of the splash of my hands coming out the water.

I looked into the water, dark red, and the monster shadow was right under me. Its shadowy claws moving like a fish, mocking me. I was way over waist deep.

Bubbles, several rolling up my spine, causing warmness to my body.

Shadow claws moving towards my body. Mind ready even in another world, where my capabilities are limited. My enemy was making me stronger. This bought on the emotion Courage.

Lights off

Pause

Lights on

I sunk, to push off the monster and to give it an unexpected surprise. The force pushes it farther to the sea floor. I would fight using my feet, I would.

This got me closer to the red light, as it blinked to a nauseating attraction.

I had to take a chance, racing towards the middle of no where, water entering my mouth. Salt was gone, fresh was in.

I move closer towards the light source, my view beginning to pick up on the background.

A little beyond the red light, the shadows of animals on all four legs, creatures were maybe wolves. The glare of their shadows produces the illusion of them standing on water.

Should I turn around, should I stop, should I keep going? My mind knew I had to do either, or. My mind was to get to the light source and gain my stableness of planting my feet on solid ground.

The area of gloomy darkness, surrounding most of my eye sight, the objects around was mystified in its own actions. The four legged creature's shadow was scratching at the top of the border, where air met water.

The monster shadow, underneath me, seems to be moving from under my feet.

Lights off

An undertow under my feet, a current forming a massive wave inside the water, I went under.

Lights on

I resurface, with a squeal to receive air. The sounds of many dogs enter my tube, the tune of heavy breathing, to my ears. The breathing of excitement, the drama of me moving closer to them, their patience was weighing thin.

The shadow underneath me was swiftly flinging backwards, away from me. Did it have no more temptation for the game or was it scared of the four legged creatures?

This thought, forward movement came to a treading to view the whole area in question.

The shadows of wolves or maybe dogs, bouncing off the water pass the red light, the caption maybe a couple of hundred feet away. I knew they weren't in the water, waiting for me to come out.

They were so close but the water height got deeper, how was they a float or was my feet about to hit the sea floor. This gave off a wary surrounding.

My mind came to grips with recognizing a survival skill, make a positive out of a negative, make it to the light and go from there. Being scared still had its placement.

Lights off

The red light shut off. The noises enter my hearing, of the wolves giggling and stumping.

Lights on

The red flashing back on from the water, something had covered it up, as a shadow rose from above it.

My body begin to stiffen up, joints in a episode of ER, my frame of mind was so lost, I didn't know if to come or go. My eyelids were ready for a closure to a blink.

My view picking up, a red honeybee, above the light, bursts out of the water, rising in the air.

It was the same size as me, wings were on fire. I went under with wondering of how to get out of this, a trap of hysteria.

Lights off

Lights on

Covers being yank from my face.

A teenager face, right in front of my face, "Get up! Read my lips Get Up!" a grin from Deborah. My lips frown, not finding a thing funny.

"Boo who, sun is out, and its time to eat," Deborah spitted in my face as she spoke.

I mugged her face back, smiling she raised her arm all the way in the air. Her hand coming back down, stuffed half a biscuit down her mouth, with little measures of chewing.

I smiled and blew up my cheeks, she was being over hyper to the taste or either very hungry.

Raising her other hand to her mouth, to present an invisible cup of drink, opening her mouth, full of biscuit and sticking out her tongue, Deborah jotted out the door to retrieve moister to the mouth.

Deborah what a complex doodle this young lady is, a teenager with a smile like no other. I knew our friendship was weird, but that's the secret decoder.

Lifting my legs out the bed letting the ray of sun, touch my temple. A welcome glance I gave as I looked out the window.

I was awake and glad of it. I wasn't sure if it was a dream or nightmare. I knew it was a thing of the past and the frighten haunting of the past.

Frustration talking to my hunger, time to eat.

CHAPTER 2

No Understanding

Tick Tock

Tick tock

My eyes open to a shooting star, bright, falling beyond the window seal.

Tick tock

Turning my head towards the noise, my eyes glanced at an owl clock, posted on the wall.

The clock had eyes, but not of an owl, of a lizard, staring.

It blinks!

The last of that star light was gone

Lights off

The darkness playing around with the thought I wasn't alone. Sleepiness could be the mirage.

Lights on

A light comes on, a distance away, a tunnel of darks as its surrounds, many feet away. The tunnel walls were a mass of nonentity, no sound, no activity, the space of nothing.

Chills started its way down my back, forming a group in single file line, the sensation running down the back of my legs.

I could tell that now I was standing not laying.

I could hear the sound of deep breathes, to my right. My eyes were searching for this sound, in the mist of the mass confusion. My eyes drift to connect with the breathing; the eyes on the clock glowing and staring at me.

Dragon!

The only thing visible was the glowing red of the eyes sockets, squinting, lower and lower, surrounded by darkness, my elbow jerk, sending motion sensors to the skin. This reaction opens my nostrils to confusion of practicing its last intake. Startle in the new format.

I need leverage, and seeing was a key. My feet feeling like flippers, as I gave way to the light.

My body flopping from side to side, in my forward movement, eyes focusing on the light and nothing else.

Breathing in my ear, I knew not to look to the side. If I did my tracks would send panic to my brain cells and a pause to my feet.

One light turns into many shiny lights in my eyes. Showers of rays enter my pupils, moving about my feet and sense of swampy wetness, building up between my toes.

My eyes creating a war against strength and weakness, telling my brain all was lost.

Lights off

Sight was a blindness and weakness. Chasing havoc with suggestions of no dragon in sight, forming congestion to the brain. My toes added infection to movement, quick sand, sealing them down; a moister that takes down slowly.

On my neck, I can feel breathing with a brush to my hair, with the sound of deceivers talking.

Whispering and sniggering, vibrating threw my sound barrier of pressure that range in my ear. My movement at a stand still.

My sight was in shock, the portrait of fright.

Lights on

I open my eyes, unfolding to a settling brightness and a refocusing.

The sounds of a stream, strong to my hearing.

Light sources under my feet, as I looked down at the surface, mind numbing but helpful. Two inches of muddy concrete presented in a cave, of dark and bright that you couldn't see the walls to the right or left.

Twisting my waist, my feet totally mount to the surface of the light. Looking for mind suggestions, but I was in the mass of darkness, around my figure.

My feet planted within the frozenness of fright.

My neck turning, my eyes forward and out of the darkness, open the eyes of the dragon. It was in two arm links away from my flesh. The eyes glowing in the darkness and I was in the light. It's looking directly at me. Could it smell the blood racing from the back of my legs?

My body wasn't a joke, having mystery told to the knees. The joints and calves being tickled with an ignorant surprise, with laughter from its eyes, my mind being taken as the jack ass.

My mind creating the art of fright.

My feet slipping from the surface, falling sideways, the red evil stare at a stand still in space. The eyes shut down from the terrifying zoom.

Lights off

The stumps of a pouncing dragon, foot coming down with a bang, as it steps followed.

Boom boom, boom booom, boom booom

Lights on

This fall captivated a pause in my sight. This clumsiness brought on the quantity of thoughts of a trap.

I'm stuck in quick sand, no more then four inches deep. This reviled a light under my feet, of mud under me. My fingertips reaching, half arm link from the top of my head, gritty wetness.

The dragon's eyes were gone.

I was on my back, sliding in to the cargo of a small cave. This chamber came within emptiness. To a place where a scream could never be heard, so the tongue, in traumatic disposition, believed the hype.

Being trapped creating a drawing, within my skull, a new strategy, gravity. My weight playing against me, the sliding infected scraping of my skin on the surface under me.

My temples at a pulse of bursting, stress in the mist of a caged migraine.

The pressure and weight sending back breaking spasms to my thighs.

Reposition a question in time, no understanding of the collapse, moaning and groaning of the muscles, gravity kicking at my rights.

The light a foggy mist.

The wet concrete puddle had a hold of my area it was touching, movement only cause myself pain. Staying still in those parts, would be a good answer, for the moment.

My face was ready to look around; my eyes were ready for no such thing.

Neck moving upwards my eyes saw mud above my face. A drop of warm slag hit my temple, and one more to the cheek. My body begins to rock side to side, revival of the skin. The brain sending waves of effective clapping to the lungs, setting off a chain reaction to the heart. The unknown taking its spot on the aisle, scream and hollering to the shoulder, causing a quiver to the root of my teeth. A circular hold injected, rapping to my brain waves, expressing being enclosed; forcing hysteria to notice-no room to work with.

I had to find the entrance; because that's the only way I got in.

In the mist of darkness above my head, I noticed "two" red dots above me.

Lights off

My body drifting away from my mind; a incredible stroke of panic tapping down my throat. My heart rate speeding, I could hear my beats in rhythm of river dancers performing their last encore.

Smmmaacckk

Landing flat on my back, the grip of my palms didn't have a chance with my weight.

Lights on

I thought closing my eyes would support the push to my palms.

As I lay, my back stuck in the mud, movement would be torture, fight against the weight of my body. I had to collect my strength, so everything paused except my eyes.

Facing the expectation of the roof, the red dots were gone.

In all directions of sight, the resemblance of a narrow swampy cave.

With the pause came a bit of courage, thinking I came in, so I can come out.

The direction to follow won't be hard but body movement would halt my escape.

The ground was muddy and slimy, warming up. The mud had it's owe purpose, to contain without force. The force would be my own struggle.

Confinement entering into my blood, with heist of new development. Exploring and creating a tide wave around the muscles. At this point, realize I had no choice but to start the moving process. Infliction to the route of patience, my body was ready, but my strength was low.

I start scooting down, using a slow butt wiggle to adjust to the fight.

The sound having its play of humorous laughter, from witches brewing over their pots. Which kept me from totally focusing; echoing sounds of brews, spells, and curses. Their laughter, an invitation to gossip. My ear drums being sent to the level of earthquakes tipping on my jaw bone causing systematic quivers.

My head sinking deeper, to cover most of my ears with mush, the quick sand was rising.

Looking around in this enclosed circular cave and a pool of force. The light showed a darker shadow of movement way passed my feet.

I decide in my mind move outward would start more rumors of the unknown, but I just couldn't keep still either.

Scoot more toward the shadow, quickly it was gone. It moved back towards where it came from.

I knew which way was the exit, by my feet, in the darkness of my surroundings. The question, could it hear my struggles of wanting relief? Was it waiting for me to come out?

A hesitation came to my crawl. The ritual was shutting down all functioning parts, in a matter of seconds. The feeling in my feet left, running to the stomach, and giving it the same pressure. An instant stop of the side to side movement, the lower torso had paused. An essences need to cooperate with the lungs. Telling the heart to sleep it off. Adding insult to injury, brainwaves started attacking each other for the last good breath, while the bad came rushing in.

Lights off

A crazed nervousness came within me, the struggle of escape created another struggle of distinctiveness of facing the enemy.

Lights on

Temporary shut down, to what's next?

My eyes and mouth came open.

Thinking it's waiting for me to come out. Sneaky! It was no way I was jus going to lay there. The swarming begins.

This time heart was the leader and it was going to shield that position. Fighting for leadership came to thoughts, it would be better to wait and build up strength. My heart, knew no time like the present. Waiting could cause laziness to the functioning of my body, which would give power to the phrase, temporary shut down. The legs could stiffen up; more focus would be in need. The back disagreement was integrated by the environment

My worm effect started to persevere, the back of the legs begin to burn. The muddy sustains became rocky and sharp, as the cave begin to widen. Realizing a pro and a con was having its tug.

Now knowing, everything is trying to stop me. I knew in my brain cells, that I wouldn't stop until I was free.

The sounds of a stream being washed away played in the background, a low volume of shaky footsteps entering into my hearing. The echoes of sound were confusing, no idea of the distances of the steps.

The lighting getting bigger, showing off an even bigger cave. My scoots turn into a slide, my body moving downwards fast, sensation of small, downwards hill.

My back and buttocks begin to burn, roughly. Pressured to seat up, no matter what the consequences. My palms down, changing me into a divesting squat

Loud POP!

My back was off the ground.

The sounds of crackles and harsh giggles, tickling at my lobes, a design of a tickle in a disturbing nature.

The light dull under my feet but I knew I had to stand up, my lower body wouldn't last another minute. The metaphor of acid pushing to the third level of torture, my skin was burning.

Pushing up wasn't the whole problem. Bear claws drawing up and down my legs to my butt cheeks. The heat was cross sketching, making it noticeable to my bones. Vibrations within the body echoing to hollowness of the mind. Dead weight, my wrists were at risk of breaking, with the help of third degree burns.

I rose to the faulty occasion.

A sensation rushing to the mouth, a long moan. Whispering of removal of pain to the elbows. Vertically the mind felt more then a moan and horizontally the wooziness carried to the bottom of the feet. Mud was coming out my mouth.

My head beginning to spin and shadows grew.

My sensation of a wave proceeding in my body, a wave of challenges of muscle over matter and that matter is gravity. Channels moving threw my toes, with the pretense of pinching, intentions of rejuvenation to the flesh, plucking now at my soles.

Glaring up the shadow had form above my face. Individuality was seen of the eyes, a certain body part with distinction.

These eyes were red as a flame, humanly.

Everything beginning to go dark, my sight was in denial. A slap of death coming into my air waves, lights blinking on and off. A shadow off my own shadow on a white wall, I felt as though I was lying down, the shadow was standing, this scaring my mind.

"ershom", I hear, from my left, partly coming in and strongly going out.

Turning my head, my eyes opened widely. The mind was at its own conclusion and sent the message to the eyes.

Lights off

Tired, the pain was a shut down with measurements of existing exaltation. My focus was strong but the weight was stronger. It was my time to go to sleep with force. This sleep was different, an amnesia in its own making. Till we meet again, I wouldn't understand the reasoning at first, but I would get an understanding of the motive, Later!

CHAPTER 3

The Prevention of Me Myself And I

Lights on

My lids flutter at the light, of red, as a trance took hold of my sight. Before or after, my memory was leaving, I could see, a shadow of a whip, flying in the air. The sounds of it hitting water as it came down.

Touching the top of my head, the ceiling was moving closer. The darkness of the room was weird. The room formulated a twist in the shadows. My face turns sideways, focus was indiscreet.

Sounds of strange groans with hidden hysteria, and a rope in motion, spinning above my head.

I see it, a shadow on the wall. The wall was dark with light from the opposite side of my face. What a filthy wall, full of rotten wood and a design of being condemned.

The shadow was huge and round; I couldn't tell what was the head or tail. Humpty dumpy was sitting on a wall.

Kaaaaaaabooooom

This sound hit my hearing, causing a general pain of confusion. This confusion was opening up my senses. Where am I? How did I get here? What's the motivation? What's My motivation! I'm going to make it threw it, hopefully.

Lights off

Taking a pause to make sure, that this show was going on, and to get ready. The tall tale of a shadowy blob wiggly on the wall and tell of tricks and trades of a rude image.

Confronting another possibility of losing my mind or controlling it. These days losing was a frame I came across one time to many.

Lights on

Taunted by the strange callings, within sound. Open my eyes to a wonderland of horror.

Lights flew pass my sight, falling stars within my side view, within the room. The room lit up right in front of my face, causing a blindness of area.

The sounds of thunder entering my eardrum to a beat of seek and destroy, instead of befriend and transform. My levels of acceptance were frozen to a point of circular subjections of shock. Territory of the muscle rushing a warm presence; locking them in a massage of panic. A heart beat coming in, pacing rapidly to a funk of unconsciousness.

Shadows dancing around my head as I look up. The wonderland was so many shadows running from the light, trailing each other. The same format but different movements, pace, and size. I could see different grins in the clouds of darkness, wildly presented in the air, being shifted one to another to another, etc. The walls of cloudy grins, jus rugged, jus condemned, jus disowned.

A rush came over my veins of hotness. I felt as though I had jumped off a ten feet bridge with no protection. A speeding lightness to my weight, squeezing at my nose, an interruption needed. Bring a push to the brain of a volcano erupting in the mist of my brain cells and I was floating at the same time.

My scale being tipped by tickles under my feet. A moment of mad laughter without a hesitation in control, riding threw my lips, presenting damage to my tongue. .

The spine joins in to feel the vibration; reaching the neck with a crisp jerk, causing whip lag with the cells in the frontal lobe. A rush of blood to the eyes and the madness begins. Lips shaking, Madness was taking its full course, not being stop by imitators. Suggestions of stop within the ear drums, ringing and ringing, but no time to stop and answer. The lungs gave a pause but no boundary for the madness.

"relief," tweeter off my lips as flashing lights were blinding me. I couldn't get focus.

The sounds effects of that word "relief", echoing and crackling in my ear.

In one of my ears, sound came to a halt, as I spun; a burst hit that lobe, smothering spring water. Coming in smooth, intention of cruel and unusual punishment, blocking my hearing. My mind being effected by the closing of sound, lunacy and misplacement are the emotions tapping in with strength.

My laughter took over my body as I spun. Channels were being changed amongst the wave of pure madness. Lights blinking boldly as I kept falling.

Swaying in the motion of a wounded fish, chills form in the core of my heart. My hearing picking up the sound of snake hissing, entrance is without invitation nor resistance.

Lights off

Shutting down to adjust my eyes to focus. My throat sent out a cough, slim came over my muscles. A slithering contraction within my veins, vibration of a creepy style. My perception of individuality was in terror of losing the battle.

My backbone getting touched by a spasm, caressing and nurturing to its effect of rapture. Life wasn't in me, a rude awaken to being conquered without dieing.

My stomach begins to growl and rumble with focus, its invisible contents getting ready to pop.

The second cough reviling an attack of my acids, building up pressure. Set on coming out of a shell of confinement.

Third quick cough and a release from my stomach muscles, dry cough of regurgitating.

Hyperventilating came to party, while temptation gives an exercise to life to quit.

Lights on

Feeling my legs, my focus was an abroad. I was outside a door in a hallway full of darkness, wrapping myself in a ball. The crack from a door produced light to a hall.

The walls oily and dirty of filth from a antique coal mine.

A crack in the door was to my left. I was not in recognition of where and how. I did notice this is a chamber, with moistness presented everywhere.

Sounds of drips and drops around my ears of water.

I focus on my feet; they were based in warm tar up to my ankle bracelet, I was sitting in it. A warming comfort to my body, a wave within of realization of the feeling, I'm alive.

A shadow fiercely runs by, coming from the crack in the door. Mouth dropped and eyes opened, the shadow processed with its own individuality into the darkness behind me.

I wasn't going into the darkness so the door was my only answer, or was it.

Getting to my feet, they slumped over to the side in the tar, as I reached for the door. The tar was unusual, no fighting for movement. Its announcement of soothing almost kept me still.

The shadows coming to a stand still, just a bright light embracing my pupils in the opening.

My eye lashes a couple of inches from the crack. I peeked making sure not to open it any further.

The floor covered with anacondas, in a thin layer of water. The creatures over lapping one another, their faces hidden, creating darkness to the wood floor in their movement. Where the light source was I could see a chair, turning my face to capture the scene. The back of someone sitting in a chair, feet folded up under their buttocks.

I knew I had to do something, I wasn't alone. Great, but how was I suppose to get the attention without causing attention to the snakes.

My hand touched the door to give it a little push. The tips of my fingers started to ache. Boiling by the nails, I felt a sensation of itchy poison ivy, with many synchronizing stings from bees.

I had to ignore the pain; these stings would not stop the quest.

My eyes balls started moving side to side, a phantasm feeling of scary of what I saw.

A mirror in front of the person in the chair; levitating in mid air, no wall to be seen. The size, 15 x 15, with light coming from the right. This reflector was surrounded by darkness. Notations placed on the mirror-mirror. The chair from the mirror, at least three arm links away.

I focus on the mirror, the back of a person reflection. The same back of the person in the chair! Glancing full throttle, the back of my - mine own body, naked. Seeing myself sitting nude towards the mirror. Fright was in existence and terror its position.

The burning reaching my elbows but consciously I had to make due.

I became mesmerized by the mirror.

Lights off

Total darkness came over the scene..

Lights on

Open my eyes to the mirror, looking in the reflection of the back of my head. Position same as the image in the chair.

Her right hand rising, rapidly above her head, the image in the mirror did it first. The seating image, mimicking the woman in the mirror, reenactment of the same story. The mirror presumption was only little above the shoulders but action showing it was the controller.

The same but different, the complexion of the skin in the mirror was bluish black.

My vision was getting the best of me. An enchant forest of misconception, enter my thoughts. My eyes travel the room of darkness to investigate. Nothing my vision could pick up, the lighting was only around the chair, beaming dully around the sitting frame. A thin ray of light coming to the door, the snakes still in motion, and their wet sound was eerie. The light concealed in front of the face of the replica of me in the chair. The chair, wooden and small, no back support, jus enough room for seating.

Her arms in the air, the reflection in cohort with the mirror. The reflection in the mirror only went a couple of inches above the head, couldn't see the hand. The figure sitting was a different story; the wrist turns no movement from her body.

She begins to open her fist, starting with the pointer finger. The one finger begins to point straight up, reviling a light switch. The pointer coming back down, the tip of this finger touching the switch, with a flick at the switch.

Lights off

Wining came to my tonsils.

Click

Lights on

Now I knew the reflection had the light in its hand and the person in the seat had the switch. I could see the light had to becoming from the mirror. She, a reflection was controlling the light.

The arm in the mirror started to turn and the double of me seating in the chair, followed the leader. The changing of the lighting, gave proof to the holder, the objects in the room grew darker, almost becoming shadows. That twist of the arm was to hide the light source in her hand.

My thoughts jumping, I couldn't enter without signing a note of verification to my insanity. Waiting wasn't the answer either.

Lights off

Hysteria, gnashing at my skin.

Lights on

The room now in a black and white version, taking color out of my sight.

I don't know, I don't know, enter the mind frame.

My eyes' getting heavier by the work out it was receiving, adjusting to the environment change of deception. A sound picking up of heavy rattling. My eyes move to the mirror, a snake coming down the arm.

The water moccasin, wrapping around her arm, as it came to the bottom of the mirror. The snake came out the mirror, stretching to the arm of the female seating. She sat still as it wrapped around her arm, she had no emotion of this terror crawling up her arm.

The snake skin turning the color of ocean blue, as it exits the mirror; it was black inside the reflection, the only thing with color in my view.

Its movement up the arm was mystifying. The snake not attached to the mirror, made its way to the top of the arm. The head turns towards me, peering in attack mode.

The arm in the mirror starts shaking back and forth, fast. The light source turning into blinks of light.

Entrance of brain confusion, my curves gave off an imbalance of rocking. The rocking was internal not ex. I was partly on the ground view that I wasn't totally standing up, I was on my knees, peeking in the cracked door.

Jumping thoughts, knowing and understanding are different. I knew it would come with a major sting; understanding of next step was vaguely staged. The clone of me on the chair arm starts to move back and forth, mimicking the mirror. This making it harder to get a grasp on the room tricks.

The mirror begins to rock on the invisible wall. The chair following, rocking as the snake came down.

I realized that I was connected to the door. The tips of my fingers were touching, and it wouldn't let go.

The snake coming my way, down the arm, now with its fangs showing, half of its body in the air ready for the sting of a bite. Its fangs growing as it touch the snakes on the floor.

Lifting half of its body in the air, walking and slithering boastfully.

Lights off

I knew it was a cheater, and cheaters never prosper. She or me, made another obstacle, planning the win.

Opinion set in, which was greater the room of darkness or the chamber. I hope I chose wisely.

Lights on

I closed the door with my other hand. Pain with death could come if I came in. I'll take my chances in this outside chamber.

The door taking another victim, the knob is covered with tiny thorns, cutting into my other fingers. With the shut, it releases my finger tips, but issued pain before release to all of the above. The door numbing something with great value to me, my fingers was of no use but a torture that is a constant reminder of agony of the skin.

With no applause I turn to find another escape. Thoughts enter in and came out with a damage of intelligences. Forget about a sting, it's time to survive, thoughts intruded.

Posed toward the cracks that gave me some light, now, back in the chamber wasn't so bad.

Turning to face my surroundings and to find out what was this hot topic. My eyes look at the cracks in the wall.

A sound came to my ears; entrance is without invitation nor resistant, of loud hissing, many and all different species.

A fog light came on low, down a ways in the hallway, blinking as it was ready to blow; now I could tell that something was beyond. The light was of no help, darkness had consumed most of its brightness. I look back towards the cracks.

Fangs, tearing into the cracks, stack on top of each other, starving for release into my area. The sounds of others behind waiting impatiently to come out, thousands and thousands of them echo in my sound. They were making a break threw of the rotten wood, the oil destroy the foundation.

I knew snakes were in the walls; my best bet was to go down the hallway.

A crack in the wall next to this split, it was dark, I stared, a black eye peeking at me. The crack covered by a body, keeping the light source in the room, watching me.

My bones felt a quiver and my legs weren't ready. The time was now.

Removing my feet, one at a time to move in the wades, towards the unknown. As I stuck with the plan, becoming three steps into the forth.

My breathing was changing, signing my self to a doom. My air passage was getting smaller, telling the heart to flat line. Interruptions from the lungs, of no air no air. Fear was having its composite to taking over.

Foolish to look back, but my instinct told me to watch the openings of the cracks, instead this brought on a dangerous fright of escape. I knew it was dark and what about those snakes.

It happens.

A part of a snake head coming out the opening. Light peeping between the cracks of the other snakes showed me a new spot light. Shadows coming out the other crack in view. My wits even knew to be scared. I had to move faster, making my legs shake in the tar.

Snakes and a shadow in this darkness, I didn't have many choices, run!

I sprint towards the light, surrounding myself with complete darkness as the light behind grew darker.

The hissing went away but a whispering was coming in above it. Whispering of chatting within another language.

Arms out, tips of both hands were touching the walls. A blind side shows nothing but evidence proved to be a hallway cover with dark clouds. Proceeding to go forward, no light behind but the light in front of me presented a show. A show of a new dimension. A hallway, I could conceive. A ring of narrowness underneath the light, the walls were caving in. My body might not be small enough to continue on, but choices were few.

My feet came in contact with a puddle, as I move forward.

Whispering turn into loud laughs of overwhelming indulgence. The hairs on my neck aroused to the laughter, sending invitation to my spine. A paralyzing numbiness was created to my knees, my heart pushing, nay nay nay to the brain. Desolation was trying to comfort but stubbornness took the platform.

Next step,

Lights off

Lights on

The light was getting short on life; its next outage might be its end. I had to move quick or else, "total darkness".

An elevator present under the light, my body won't fit; the walls were closing in sections. Four feet away, as my shoulders were touching the wall. I turn my head sideways and peering down the snakes were coming, shadows by my feet at a distance traveling close.

Hissing was coming in to feed.

Pushing my body threw the narrow passage. The light was ready to go.

Lights off

Lights on

My finger made it to the elevator button it open and three buttons produced light within. I had to turn sideways; my back and chest touching the walls, in order to slide threw. The hissing was becoming loud.

I hit the elevator button as my last leg came in.

The door closing at my heel as a snake jumped in the air, not a moment to soon.

Glancing quickly, a regular old Otis, the buttons gave off little light. As my heart rate went down, my thoughts were "a little is appreciated to the fullest."

I hit 1, even though I had hit B earlier, and shock went threw my finger. Knowing it was from pain earlier and wetness from my hand was electrifying. Waking my sight up, noticing the whole elevator with cause.

Elevator old and rusty, spider webs in the corners, a burnt smell in the air.

Trying to ignore what I smelled, I embraced my self for another trip around the scantiness of signature rapture. I was regretting the turn of observation that I knew I had to look around to view all my surroundings.

My mind being block by sight, looking at my hands first, they started turning blue black. I knew then I was in trouble. The other hand balled up within itself.

A brush to my hair causes a jerk to my neck, creating a tear to roll down my cheek. The roots of my hair were on fire, a burning pain within the skull, causing a different explosion.

My realization of what, looking to find no answer yet.

Muscles flexing for the fight, every last one of them ready, excising to a rhythm less nature. My esophagus whistling to the tonsils, with a breeze of expression.

With a push to the tongue, a very eerie scream.

Looking at the corner of my eyes, covered with madness, and caught a shadow jumping back into my shadow within this small compartment. Arms of a shadow coming around with an impression of grabbing. My body reacting without a moments notice, slinging my arms out to show my shadow didn't want this, refusing this embrace.

Tumbling of the mind as the nerves begin to collapse. Refusing to say it is but noticing it, created falseness to my bare feet. Numbness stereotyping my environment, coming up with its own conclusion. The conclusion that it was something pushing and shoving at my mentality to levels that need readjusting. Hyperventilating made itself known in this passenger crate.

A hard jerk in the elevator and the doors started to open. I wanted out of the elevator, a lost cow in the wilderness. The placement and settings were all wrong.

A sound of laughter pierced my ears. A crackle giggle, with an aftermath of division. Separating the waves threw the sockets and the temples of pressure. I froze as the doors came open. Noticing breathing on my neck, a flowed came to the eyes. The skin under the back hair line rushing the pain of pressure. Pressure in the form of chills of fright.

Lights off

Not the doing of my out side vision, but put by an inside sight. A shove to my back, pushing me off balance out the elevator.

Lights on

The shove stops my fainting with a slap, with the attention, back on, breathing.

Leaned against the wall, a rage took its spot on the tonsils, pushing out air. Jumping into the heartbeat of simple madness.

Brightness administer rapidly to my eyes, as if to be looking directly in the sun, as it takes my sight.

Lights off

I had to turn it off, this light brought pressure to the brain of nothing to focus on. A stain of pushing sight farther, but everything was too amazing.

I step forward even with my lids close, I could see sparkles of light. My feet begin to slide and I could feel myself slipping as my eyes came open.

The sound of a stumbling horse, hearing "-me-"coming in rudely and leaving out fast. Noise came to a stop, dead in its tracks a halt.

Lights on

Hands waving back and forth in front of my face, in a weird saxophone effect. Saying something, but I couldn't comprehend.

They were blurry and little waving in my face.

Lights off

It was time to sleep or wake up.

CHAPTER 4
Come To Grips

My thoughts knowing I wanted out from this illusion. It's time to see the problem and come to grips.

With mind suggestions I finally Open-my eyes.

A little girl faces, in my face. My face looking towards the ground, I was sitting, as she passes by me, catching each other eyes.

She was of Hispanic descent, black hair shiny. She could have been seven or a little eight. The eyes round like pearls, with the enter color cherry wood and amber. Her eyes staring, in mine, the sinus of a burning stare.

Lights off

A blink in thoughts, thinking I must be daydreaming.

Lights on

I'm in a room, looks like a clinic and three tall windows on the right. The windows were appetizing to my eyes and the rest was space and opportunity. Behind the glass on the outer side, a security badge swapper and an envelope slot at the bottom of a window.

Turning my neck, more to the left, a plain wall, and no pictures no emphases. Contrasting more with this slow turn, two rows of chairs by the glass door, five to each row.

The turn end on a plain wall and one big window.

Not a human in sight, where's the girl.

A voice spoke, "you are not alone." A sound effect of vocals turning into harps.

I stood up to get a visible conversation coming from anywhere.

None.

Shadow appeared in the room coming from the door. I paused and inhale. My eyes getting ready for the focus to see this host of the shadow.

An elderly Spanish woman maybe late seventy and the little girl holding her hand, walking pass me, in this room. The little girl head turns toward me, she's now staring.

Lights off

Her eyes burning my view, again.

My lids blink constantly until the lights in the room came back to focus.

Lights on

The little girl walking, straight in front of me, I could see the back of her, as her neck turn to keep the stare. Her feet had a glass reflection, too much sunlight on the shoes, kept it a blur. The shoes made out of mirrors. The harpy sounding voice announced, "You are not alone."

I had to keep caption, the shoes took my thoughts for a second.

The shadow of them walking towards the door is my view.

My ears knew what direction the sound came from. My feet begin to move fast, I had to catch them.

Opening the glass doors to find the shadows owners.

Touch the rail to the glass door sent my body to another zone. My hand nabbing up as though electrical shock of cold air, reaching in quickly threw the tips of the fingers. Spreading to joints, hitting up the blood for leadership. Stopping at the palm, itch within the right hand of an itch that could never be scratch.

Stepping out of the door, quickly my feet was stuck in muddy concrete. I could see the shadow far in distance

My vision, long for adjustment and none came. In sections my vision could see, the first section to the far left, was moving in a wave, one direction, parking lot. The second and third section, shaking and vibrating to the left, building and more cars. The feeling of funny mirrors, but no mirrors, jus space and opportunity, to put notice on the shadows.

I begin to wave my arms, fatigue was here, and was delight of the spotlight. Cut no boundaries of being notice, coming threw the tips of my gut, as nasty chills and releasing a boom in my system starting with the eyes.

I could see their shadow at a distance standing straight on the ground while the area around it moves in this third dimension frame. I started shaking as the shadows disappeared quickly.

I had to change my mind into getting back in the building; outside my vision was making me sick. The rails on the door were gone, a door with no entrance from outside, jus an exit.

Looking threw the doors I could see, movement.

A sound came to my ears "always there," brushing against my face, like a wind from the tonsils but blowing like a fan. My eyes were in need of moisture, now with a time out.

Lights off

This is serious, why does these dreams or day dreams, play around? Knowing I will wake up. Am I sleeping or is this really happening?

My heart rate move at no rhythm, causing my senses to-

Lights on

My eyes were already open, jus as if I was staring into space.

Inside the building I was still sitting down and the little girl is sitting with the elder lady on the chairs in front of me. The area they were in was darker then my area, but I could see enough this time.

Their bodies and chairs were at a slant; I could only see the head of the elder lady and the little girl the side of her face and body her legs swinging moving fast back and forth creating a dark slide show. She turns her face towards the doors, staring straight at me.

I could see her mouth barely moving.

Trembling in my ears, jumping off echoes. Following and leading to a sound of its own tune, creating echoes within echoes.

Putting my hands to my ears to cover up some of the sound, other senses were ready for a break but I refuse to break but at the same time, I did.

Lights off

"siempre hay," sounded off into the air wave killing all other sound, with a embracing of courage. This harp had its own beat and gain strength from being the lowest and bravely coming in boastfully.

Lights on

My head shaking off the blank stare. My veins wanting to snap out of it, pressure to my temples. The reflection of dangerous muscles flexing in a worm movement threw my shoulders, force relaxation to the neck.

I start to receive a warm sensation crawling up my skin.

A little girl laughter coming in with a bang to my drums, high pitched and very disturbing. For a few seconds and then silence again.

It was raining above my head. I look up and the bulb was broken but still shining. Looking back down and a shadow was in the corner, dark and hidden. My eyes pops in the sockets, a fright of distinguish torture.

I jumped, and a splash came to my feet, not of hearing but feeling.

The water hitting my leg like boiling water, a blister to the hair follicles. The shadow started coming out centimeter by centimeter.

The horrifying giggle coming in, with a pitch that was unheard of.

Lights off

I could feel my self shaking, darkness giving me a big scare. The light went out.

"Always there," the sound of a bell hit hard by a hammer, the ringing made the words not vocals.

Lights on

The broken light came on to a dimness of little but noticeable light.

The glass wall in front of my face was filling with water. Everything inside the building was being engulfed by a tidal wave. Black shadows of birds diving into to the waters surrounding, none came back up.

The water level over taking the seats, the room containing the water.

The glass door came open.

My body getting hit with a tornado and winds of a hurricane; making fear turning into a Tsunami. An earthquake of misplacement, lost cattle in the middle of the swamp. My city being torn, by swarming fishes, racing in my blood. Scared and more scared, was not a question for asking. So terrified, I knew that this would end. I had to Believe.

Torn was the right word, floating thorns in the water. I press myself against the glass wall, to put my body at stiffness to movement. I had to stand all the way up, now, the water was rising. The thorns caught my leg, under water flowers of roses as I looked at the water many petals floating, in the darken sea.

The water level was rising not decreasing, the room a running faucet and I was outside the pouring bowl.

The water was growing deeper, waves slapping my face with a snap. I'm ready to slay and eat. Madness now coming in to play, this emotion was ready to dance.

Its rushing out move-move. My mind was wondering about survive, as the underwater thorns only pierced the left side of my leg.

Thinking move into the darkness, I had no choice.

Walking deep into the darkness, the thorns were no longer in my skin, but the water was up to my chest and rising. Cold in one step and hot in another, sending temperatures of ferrous hail hitting me on top of the head, the size of quarters. The shock of the coldness could turn black hair grey.

Deep enough now to swim, I could see swirls touching the air, giving the water a lightly glow.

Kaaabooom, a strong sound behind me.

A bolt of electrocuting lighting coming from another angle, directly in my sight in front of me, threw the building.

Lights off

As I trended in the water, I couldn't see a thing, sitting duck with no where to run. The waves catching my breath going over my head. Trying not to inhale the pollution, spitting the water back out of my mouth. The channels ripping threw my body with infectious bacteria causes of no effect to it, but satisfaction in destroy. Hyperthermia doing the tango with 110 degrees Fahrenheit.

Lights on

Lighting hit again, same spot, blinding. The level over gulf the building, I was in the middle of a sea. My eyes came to focus on the moon what little light it care to share.

The moon was red with the lighting of several navy blue sheers wrapped around it. It made my hands look flaming blue.

As I was trending, something long coming out the water. Many thousands of little shadows within the water of fish, around me. Strong armed, couldn't win this one, my body realizing most of it was caught in another world. This world breathing would be hard, and so my eyes showing my madness, within. My madness keeping me woke, to get to the bottom of this, reference to staying on top-of the water. My breathing changing with the bite to my mind, interference, touching rudely to my hair line, a jerk to the neck, my eyes refocused.

Sound of trumpets weeping in the form of horns. I had to keep trending and let the sound have its way.

A seahorse rising to the top of the water, floating on the top, full body. The sounds were coming from its mouth.

As clear as it was seen, even quicker it went back under, sinking and so did the sound.

My hands getting numb, my thighs at a different temperature.

I begin to feel a lift to my body of not floating but a restraint of surrounding control.

My body got stuck in an under tow, instead of pulling me under, twisting me around to where my face was in and out of the water opposite times of my feet.

The seahorse was the thing I saw with the first turn, sinking in the water, to where my eyes couldn't see beyond that darkness. Head lifted back into the air, pulling in as much as possible.

The second turn the air bubbles coming toward my face.

Within my world, the moon got dark with the first turn.

The second turn into air, I was embracing a sideways wave, coming directly at me.

My face going back under, the back fin of a big shark, underneath my frame with this spin.

Lights off

The moonlight had left.

Lights on

Lights in my blurry vision, I was being dragged in the water, by something, digging into my arms as I felt the sea floor, sand was felt on my buttocks.

Loud screaming heard within the background, as air enters my lungs. I wanted my eyes to focus; struggle was gone out of me. I went with it.

Movements of blurriness about me, cause my mind to slip.

Lights off

I fainted into the scream within my ears.

CHAPTER 5

Mirrors Mirror On The Walls

I woke up seating in a chair, a mirror right in front of me.

The room, what an enchanting forest to the eyes. The smell of roses swaying to my nose. A vanity was in front of me; in the mist of a dark circle. Around the frame of the mirror were six light bulbs, two on top of frame, and two on each side.

The beam was rather low, the watts lesser than a black light. The rest of the room empty to objects as darkness surrounded my enter circle. I was in the middle of a room, or was I?

Looking into the mirror, my hair was done up, with burgundy lipstick on my lips. The background fogged out. Checking out the accessories looking deep in the mirror. The face of a shark begins to glow in the background.

The bull shark with a smile of angrier. I turn around quickly; it had to be behind me.

Lights off

Turn my neck with a jerk cause a sharp pain of blindness. Blood red shot threw my eyes, lights off, but still seeing, only red, too much strain in the turn.

Lights on

Snowy blood slush in my eyes, trying to get comprehension, as something dipped on my face.

I felt a sickness as if I were naked on a stage in front of millions of convectors. My face arousing to the skip of madness beginning to realize something was turning on and off a switch to the cavity of my brain. The pressure at the temple was closing in smashing the skull. Delusions were set in their ways, but my mind didn't have all the options. Other senses creating a fix like no other, a fix of touch, and smell, handling wouldn't come easy.

I knew that I would conclude this mess of the brain to an end of this door being shut. Realizing enough is enough.

Starting to turn back towards the mirror, my eyes only seen a cloudy red influences around me, a layer behind my mask. I could feel something else was their but what.

I knew this wasn't true jus like the other quick flashes, or creative daydreams. How to come out, what was next, my thoughts turning into something else restructure. The brain of hardness and the body of hidden agendas. Chills were at its max, and I thought it was me making the thriller, but so I thought.

My eyes reaching the mirror, the vision of me with red hair and black lipstick, smiling. I knew I didn't have red hair, black was my color, the lipstick set me back in thought. My eyes covered with black eyeliner, on thick and dark, my eyes looked sunk back in my head.

A shadow coming up behind me in the mirror, surfacing out of the darkness, right in the back of my head.

The mouth of a cloudy shark with teeth of shining steel, coming sideways toward my head, sharp and ready to stake.

As it came down, my reflection frowned, and closed her eyes.

I was in a daze of what to do, what to do.

Lights off

I didn't know what to do but wait in pure darkness for my eyes to come alive. Sick and tired of this vision of me, she or it had to stop playing with me. Angier getting built up, my change was coming fast. I was the only one that knew about me and if this isn't me what is it? I wanted out. My hand balling up a fist, as I stood up in this darkness.

A sound creeping up in the darkness, erck erck, a walk from a monster of a weird kind. The sound coming in rapidly, ercK ERCK, I could hear the sound of its movement and body. The ground start moving with the steps of this sound

Lights on

Her lids started to open bring light into the bulbs on the mirror frame.

She's staring and laughter start stirring in the air.

ERCK ERCK, a shadow coming up to her and shaking my world, while hers was at a stand still.

Glancing at the side of my eyes, trapped around darkness.

My neck started a traffic jam, to all senses. The feet getting numb, my hands are getting hot, and head getting small. The jam of surprise, the unhelpful instructor of losing self control.

I swung into the mirror with one fist, saving the other for back up, if damage occurs.

Shattering of glass with the sound of shingles hurting the ears.

Lights off

Lights on

Two light bulbs the rest broken, one to the left and one to the right. The shadow of me, walking into view sideways in the broken, but not scattered mirror, it seems the top of the hair was bright red and rest dark as the background. Walking sideways bought a shake to my head.

Light off

I was getting ready to hit the mirror, again, shut down for protection of my eyes.

I could hear glass scrapping around me. The sound getting eerier and eerier.

Lights on

Four tall mirrors surrounding me, covering every corner to form a box. The light was directly above my head, coming from the sun, a reflection. It was a mirror above my head. The reflection from another mirror which gave a different position, this mirror was 5 feet by 5 feet above my head, but dark clouds surround it. The same size as the mirrors that caged me. The sun beaming bright from somewhere to the east, it seemed. The look of a distance gives interest to the thoughts in my mind, quickly, "Dark above my head around this mirror. What's holding it up?"

In and out went that thought, the sun was moving which gave little time in the mirror before it was gone. The mirror was the lid to the box, a hundred feet above my head.

Thoughts swift quick to survival mode, let me use what little time with this light, instead of why, and change the where. Where can I get an opening?

The mirrors had the picture of me looking up. Looking back towards the mirror in front of me, to see what's behind me.

Drops of blood on my face, and dark redness to the other side. My hand was bleeding, and dipping blood unto the floor in a puddle. The puddle was building around my feet on a wood floor. The floor was covered in blood.

Taking off my shirt and wrapping my hand, the reflections did the same. Making a fist to tighten the pressure, with the last wrap, tucking with stiffness.

The sun was moving fast and it was almost gone and I knew what was next.

Looking forward, my fist that was wrapped up came forward. The reflection put one of her arms up over her face.

Shattering came to the ears, as my eyes shut down for a second as a protection and I did the same as the reflection.

Lights off

Closing my eyes

Lights on

My reflection still was in front of me, in a cracked mirror, its look was exactly like me, no differences in this reflection. The light in this box came different; distortion came from the measurements of light. I understood now, the shattering was above my head.

The mirror was gone above my head, to show proof that the sun was not a reflection, but right behind the mirror, surrounded by dark clouds. It wasn't a mirror above my head, but see threw glass. I begin to shake the glass off my shoulders.

I turned my neck, forward, back to seeing the perception of myself.

My exact presumption of me, except she was smiling, the body in the mirror starts to turn. Her hand was double the size of mind, in the darkness within her world, a shadow approaching behind her in the mirror.

I swung again, saving the other hand from collateral damage, the back up.

Shattering hit the ears hard, cause a blindness of pain.

Lights off

Lights on

Quickly my sense with drew from the noise, silence.

The mirror begin to crack as pieces fell down, letting the surrounding darkness drop its guard. The light shining a little brighter.

The mirror was thin as a paper, sliding down and breaking in front of my eyes.

The balance of the other mirrors, were based off all four connection. The support system was broken.

A domino effect a chain reaction, it need strength from all, one breaks all breaks.

My senses were at attack, ringing of loud slamming of glass. The sound causing a stumble of my balance, eroding the eardrums, the beat setting a pattern for chimes of shivery. Harsh beats from tender kinds, sound giving me a shake rattle and roll of the nervous system.

Lights off

I wanted out of this nightmare and I wanted no more of these scenes. My mind trying to wake up, but if not I would find the answer with this one. My ears wouldn't take to much more.

Lights on

Open my eyes, fully, all the pieces of the mirrors resting on the ground, surrounding my feet. Dipped in blood and reflecting parts of the sunlight creating a glooming atmosphere.

The sun almost to its next destination, as the dark moon came over half of it, so I had to act quickly. The sun peeking on my far east.

Eye viewing, stuck in another region, a swamp, many slumped trees and linen of moss, in my view.

My view looking farther and every thing look farther. I realized I was trapped in a bigger ring of mirrors connecting. I was stuck inside of a bigger capsule. Tall mirrors, top edge mixing with the dark sky, couldn't make out the end. Darkness played a big part of hiding the height.

The twist of the feet and turning of my body, giving room but little time, the sun exiting to its daily ritual.

My train of thought confused about the wrong thing, why it couldn't stay over time? The switch of my mind, came on, It never does, its daily cycle, is always on a schedule, no matter what.

Thoughts went back to focusing as my feet sinking in the slash, the mirror disappearing in the floor of this four inch swampy bloody pool.

My step was weird, almost losing my balance, nothing to grip. The trees were two steps away, and four steps behind, the mirror giving off more trees than meets the eye.

Sounds are coming into my hearing.

The sound of a hissing snake and rattling of the thin branched trees towards the back of me.

Stepping with the other foot, darkness grew behind the trees, taking away the mirrors, to a pitch of black.

Wondering if I wouldn't wake up, to be stuck without armor was becoming a horror. My eyes wanted a shutdown; the disagreement came from the throat. A breath coming in with a fight.

Loud hissing taking over the drum.

One tree in front of my view, and a shadow came around it. A shadow growing, slyly, as the sun got covered up by a cloud. This produce a gloomy light of fog with in the air.

I took a step forward; I could hear glass breaking underneath my feet.

The shadow of a snake, behind the tree, behind me, whirls. My eyes looking back the shadow was six feet tall, standing, wings out darker than the darkness. It was sneakily making its way to me, in the corruption of the darkness; I was still under a little light.

I turn to the right and begin to run, to the lighted area, notification of it being brighter than where I was. I knew darkness was its winning, so I would try and stay clear of it.

The steps gave balance of solid ground, but stones creating pain for my arch. I knew my feet were made for walking so I had to stay on it.

The light, indulgences to my appetite to absorb, feeding into my eyes without caution. A thin line of light, sufficient to seeing something.

A touch to my left arm, a chill of red hot lava to the hairs, my eyes glanced and the snake shadow coming for me.

I made it pass one tree, and breathing was coming back faster.

A shadow coming over me, hitting my side view, moving beside my shadow. The lights in front of me, was almost gone, it was ready, trying to overcome the small light source.

My journey as I moved saw something shiny by the tree roots, in front of me.

CHAPTER 6

Get A Grip

I reach over to my right with my left, got a grip of it tightly, with the good hand. The light reflecting on it took my sight, thinking it could be a piece of the mirror and I could use it as a weapon.

I grab it and begin to swing it into the air; movement was still in process, taking the weight of the mud off it. The glare coming off the legs of a chair, jus a piece of metal shining on it. The rest of the chair full of rust and the seat and back of it, missing. I could tell critters live on it. The grab was a snatch of no boundaries. The insects and bugs on it keep it from being cover with moss and fungus, jus enough. Their gluttony and feast would give me extra power.

The Shadow grew close; I could hear the hissing directly in my ear.

My mind had to know this is a dream, so fixing itself, from the art of hearing, to bring on seeing.

I threw the chair forward with all the strength of fight in me, way into the darkness. A wisdom of survive hitting in my cells. The light was leaving in front of me, and mirrors kept it hidden. Its time for freedom to save my mind.

The crash of glass in an effect of sound waves travel many miles and could still be heard.

I paused in the mush, shattering glass flying everywhere. A party of glass, a dress code of red, and the music of cutting effects. Small pieces sprinkling, like bullet fast, the tact was my face surveying, my eyes. Hopefully no more mirrors of cages, let me be free.

Lights off

A normal reaction to the sound in route and common protection of the eyes.

Shattering glass settle down, crashing water came into to play.

Lights on

I unfolded my arms coming across my face and hands moving away from my ears bringing my arms down, slowly. I open my eyes, adjusting my view to the caption of a waterfall.

The environment was getting dark, the sun was gone, and giving my self, less than eight minutes and darkness would have its full control.

I thought not to look back, it is what it is, and the shadow of the cobra could be gone, light source was different.

The environment, shadows hiding behind the trees and a fall several feet away, and a big rock stood in the middle as the stream went around. The greenhouse picture came close to mind. In the middle of this swamp a waterfall three stories tall and then I would be out of this ditch. I could climb the side of the rocks. The sun had climb over this mountain for the day and it was time to take the shine to a different location, floating over the mountain the last of that shine fell behind the fall. I'm running to the light source that would be beneficial to the eyes of protection.

A glossiness of the surface, my eyes couldn't tell if mirrors were presented further back. I really didn't care, I jus wanted to wake up.

The walk to the fall was an acre away.

I start my journey; the glass under my feet was sinking into the ground. I felt like I was chasing the sun, staying in the light would help my defense and it was over the hill of water.

A tree starting wading to my left, stepping forward I decided to pick up a piece of glass, since the chair was behind me. Bending down a wobbly reflection in the thin layer of water of red headed me, I picked the broke mirror. Curiosity of my looks was out; using this for protection was in. I held it to my side and processed, I wanted out.

I used the bandage hand to pick it up, the covering would protect if it was too sharp.

The trees in front on my left moving violently, I could see eyes glowing behind the tree, three trees from me.

The eyes mean and viscous, a recap on this one, big and a déjà vu, that was memorable.

The Dragon!

It's in the darkness, time to run.

My feet splash as I run to the waterfall.

Breathing and stomping, I could feel it in my ears and the steps were shaking my ground. Staying to my left in front, the trees movement giving the hint.

I moved more to my right and kept straight. The water was getting deeper, a stream, connecting to the river.

I could see shadows coming behind me; I put the mirror to trial, to see behind me, towards my feet.

Sounds of many jowls eating and rapid movements, something small but many which had its own beat. I turned my head, baby crabs surrounding the back of me, covered with shadows. Could they smell the blood on my body, or were they jus hungry.

The noise of my moment must have woken them up, they were slower than me but that means I could slow down a little to caught my breath.

A loud laughter from a hyena taking over the sound, coming from the right of the woods.

This laughter came in and left, returning the sound of the crabs, and rumbling of the ground from the dragon.

Now I'm at a swim or I could run the side of the river. The choice was interrupted.

Four shadows of wolves lining up at the edge to the left, darkness was falling. Everything was hungry and my flight into the other side created much noise.

The water grew taller with every step that I got closer to the rock. The start of a swim to the rock, with my mirror still at hand.

The rock, I could use it to get to the sides and climb the side of the water that was falling. I would be at the top, but troubles were causing another defect. What were the troubles over there, and the sun was almost gone. I realize it's a dream and I'm supposed to keep trying, no matter what.

Swimming I reached the rock, taking a look back; the shadows of the crabs were at shore, clawing at the wolves shadow.

Within hands reach of the rock, it was a boulder.

Sliding back in the water I couldn't get a grip. I place the mirror above my head and grab again. No luck

I need a good look at the rock and notice it had more loop holes around the back as the water poured behind it.

My trending around the back and a shadow appeared underneath me.

The water now blue, a shark fin.

Staying close to the rock, it was a bull shark; several feet away clear as day.

The sounds in the air, taking my breath. I knew I was getting too excised in the wrong way. My heart was ready to run, my lungs were ready to quit, and my ears were ready to kill. The mind was ready for the big ending.

I made myself get on top of that big stone, so I could at least cover my ears, the noise was murderous.

The noise of a forest gone crazy.

Out of the water, now looking around was darkness and a little light left above. I grab my mirror, putting it in my mouth, locked in placed by my teeth. I thought I might be in need of it at the top.

I stood on it to begin the climb

I took a step and grab, my left hand going into the darkness of the rocks, and processed to climb. The climb was short almost at the top, as a black whip tied around my hand, in the darkness. The grab wasn't tight but its hold was mind blogging.

Reflex, I took the mirror out my mouth and came down harshly.

HISSSSSSSS

Cutting the whip from the owner, as it released, it was the tongue of a snake. It dropped into the water, along with the mirror. Two splashes and the blue of the water turning red. Several feet down, I could see a shadow, the shark, going towards it.

I knew I couldn't fall; it was waiting for a mistake.

Making my way to the top, in about six minutes. The rocks slippery, if one won't one will, my hands had my back. A slip of one and a catch from the other, my feet were in tune with the progression.

I looked beyond the waterfall, mountains and trees, and the river was opening up.

My knee on the upper ground, dragging my other leg, I looked down.

What I saw next, took my sight.

The shark shadow moving and waiting, but a dark creature on its back, standing up. I wipe my eyes in disbelief, a dark robe of black and it wouldn't lift its head.

The shark shadow disappeared under the long black velvet robe, swaying in the water, as the robe darkness turn the blue dark. The hooded robe was unknown what was underneath, but I knew, the same one pointing its finger with a twirl. Melting into the water, change the appeal of blue to a bland black.

Hurling into the air, the shark as it rapture threw the ghostly robe, the big black snake in its mouth. It lands back in the water without a splash.

My focus came back up to my surface my body on top of the cliff. Red eyes looking straight into my mind.

Lights off

That flash sent a water storm of fire to my eyes, without the heat, jus the code red of external blindness. My eyes blinking trying to get a view.

"Siempre hay," heard with a tremble of clarinets, violating my hearing. The sound giving chills of plucking out my earlobes. The veins in them were going to bust.

Lights on

The moon the light source, dull, but using what it could get from the sun to help out my eyes to see.

The sounds of strong winds and whispers of confusion, everything around me foggy. My joints were departing from the fingers, my toes feeling alone, in the drama. The mind begins to rock, back and forth, to a beat of dumbness. Clueless to my legs floating in the liquid, and my hands on sand. Which way to go?

At the edge of the fall, the moon, fading in a camouflage.

A shadow in the water, of a wave moving towards me, growing and glowing a few feet away.

I turn to see it fully with my eyes giving full prescription. The wave giving me dribbles of cleansing and closure of ending up at the bottom of the sea. The wave would push me back down the waterfall into the shark and its back rider.

The wave getting high, staying right under the moon as it moves closer.

I look toward land, and started to get to my feet.

The surface part of my vision was many trees of darkness with humps showing, a mountain farther that way. The shadows of darkness, beyond the eyes.

The other side produced a lake of darkness and a mountain further in the unseen, of a dark lump in the ocean, roaming in the mist of crazed darkness.

My left foot touched land, the earth was moving, and I look directly at the wave. Gliding on the surface as if to be walking, spreading as it moved on dirt, creating a football line up made up of one wave.

My eyes my eyes, this wave moving on earth and water, not losing speed or height. The lights flashing threw the wave of deem blinking stars, ready to fall.

I had no choice but to drop to my knees, this dream was getting the best of my comfort zone.

I bent my head down not knowing the outcome.

Lights off

Exalted, I had to relax jus for a second and collect my thoughts. The travels of understanding becoming way too much to comprehend.

Lights on

I open my eyes

CHAPTER 7
the Amazon of H2O

Water splashes on my face, a flow that held on to this area.

The wave right in front of me, I was at the edge of the drop down.

The wave march in place, not moving forward, inside the wave something different. The show of someone standing within it, an invisible brace to the eyes.

The sound of squealing and wooing barricading my ears, smashing down, with a hint of popping bubbles.

A feeling of trying my patience, hit my liver, I knew this was another mystery in my boundaries. I didn't want to cross it either.

I took a step back, water now rising to my ankles.

A seahorse coming into to view, floating to the top, and begin surfing and riding the wave. Disappearing with a fade of retraction to my sight.

A wind forming in the middle of the wave, right in front of me, a tornado evolving.

I took a half step back.

The water filling up to my knees, sending a chill of I'm in the water. The land could not be seen, as the water rose. Retracting from forward movement, its sow of intimacy was reaping at the bottom of my spine.

I could hear the sound of strong wind and vomiting from thunder.

I thought, I had to get to land or else the fall of darkness would be a pit of blind misjudgment.

I took that step to the left, closer to what I remember was land. The tornado was spinning faster in the wave, blowing my wet hair sideways. The noises enter my ears from the wind, a trap for the tornado within the lobe.

Another step, I knew the next step would put me touching the side of the wave.

I had to choose a route, either forward or towards the bottom of the cliff, and I knew the sun was gone and the moon was at its last flicks, getting ready to peek at the next horizon.

The moon glowing threw the wave, as a dark cloud begins to have its way. A tainting of intrusion of mentally destroying any view of light I could suck up. My mustard seed of control was not defeated.

I begin to stretch my hands out so I could get a head start, before my feet came into play.

Finger tips touch the wall of water, and a quick yank back, was a normal reaction.

Something touching the tips of two fingers, a sensation of a burning chill.

The sound of a whistle humming coming in, creating, an incredible agitation to my examination.

I reach a little and I was yank into the middle of the tornado in the middle of the wave. I couldn't close my eyes, amazed at my situation. I was at the same level as the top of the waterfall but I looked down I could see the boulder. I was spinning in the middle, a dizziness of a dozy hold, taking its toll on my eyes in the twisted lake.

I was levitating in the middle; as it moves toward the bottom of the waterfall and way pass my head. That means everything down there, could spin up.

I was trapped in this arena of aqua. I was tried and sleepiness was relieving that, so its time to wake up. NOW!

Lights off

A dose off, with my thoughts, not this way.

Rubbing my eyes, water splashing as it bounces off my nose.

Lights on

The spin was stopping, my body placed at sea.

I look into the area, a watery sculpture, appeared next to me.

The water gave it a fake look of sci-fi, but realistic enough to carve into a clone of me. Was it a reflection from the lit of the moon?

The figment is getting its own pose, as if it was ready to jump out the water.

I begin to kick my feet in fright of this unknown, my arms joined in as I begin to swallow water.

It grabbed my hands, smacking down on the surface, yanking me in.

How do you fight water?

My body want into a dolphin spin, as I could hear, "You don't."

I shut down and went lifeless. Keeping my energy and last breath for reservation until the end. I couldn't beat it, so struggle was useless, it enjoyed the fight. My thoughts stayed open to observing my next move, a second closer.

Lights Off

I couldn't see anything under water. I tried to grab at the hands that had pulled me under, how in a world without walls. I could feel water rushing around me; I was now in this spin hold. The fingers of water coming around my neck, as my head came out the water.

Lights On

The hold came off my neck, as my shoulders resurfaced.

Air; hit my nostrils like a love like no other. I was floating, as if I were dead, looking at a quarter red moon. The moon wasn't a quarter it was full, the rest hidden behind the mountains.

The wave was gone, I was floating on levelness. Cutting my eyes to the left I could see the shadow of a tree, probably at a distance several hundred feet. These measurements brought on the weight of inching gallons of hate. The shore look close, on my down time, I knew, it was longer than it look.

Should I swim or float, wasn't sure of everything around me, and I would surely wake up a new flow. The flow could transform a peace of mind and make it complex, which could change into pieces of my mind.

The thought got changed, quickly.

I started swimming. A sharp poke in the middle of my chest, and a dragging undertow was yank at my hair, building strength to pull me under.

I knew, it couldn't touch outside of the water, H_2O was its enemy.

The land of fluid, a monster seeking entrapment. The forest of a maze of mystery with darkness, in the middle was me. The sea had no emphasizes, the other trap.

My battle was getting to shore even when darkness was more in that area, it was still an advantage. I could fight better without having to fight to breath, used as an odd torture.

I took off fast knowing this creature was under me.

The wind having its way with sound in a whirly scream.

A pinch to my nose and a twist effect, the same at my arm pits. A choke of a grip came under my neck to close off the esophagus. I felt a pain of desertion, of my air pipes.

My head breaking away with a shake, barely out the water, trying to caught a breath. Nostrils in full motion, shutting down the corruption, flowing threw the mouth, from the water. Trembles, air rapidly changed in lungs. In and out, my chest jumps with no rhythm, hands joining the frustration, giving off a beast stroke.

In the wind sounds of laughter of amusement and arousing confusion, the mirage of spasms tickling down my back.

Getting close to land as I swam, I was progressing. My feet were now touching the bottom, darkness two or three feet in front of me, the moon darkening, jus enough shine to let me see around myself. The trail of darkness grew around me, my intellect knew, that something was up.

I was doggie paddling to where I could stand without breathing difficulty.

I couldn't see the ocean floor, but I was standing on something slippery. I lift my feet up to swim instead of walk, even though the confusion got the best of my energy.

I was to close to losing it now; I had to get to shore, in a format of protection, and to place myself on a land of my culture. Breathing wouldn't be a problem against the ocean.

SSSPPPLLAASSSHH

Something jumping out the water, behind me, I keep forward without a glance; nosiness would help entice the mood. A change of weird hope in the mist of this torture chamber.

A splash came to the side of me, maybe two feet, I glared, the shark fin. Poking out the water, I know now it was challenging me, maybe not even hungry, jus waiting to toy with me. This toying was not fun, it was dangerous.

Chest deep in the foul water, I didn't pay attention to the fish. I realized it had to come and get me, and my hands had power of self defense with stableness. "The eyes", I thought loud within me. The eyes would be painful in any species if pulled out.

My waistline touching air, I was close. I picked up speed, to land, I must go.

SPPPLLAASH

To my left, an uncomfortable tease of influence, it knew I knew it was out there but did it know I would fight, feeling the water and under waves.

Finally getting familiar with the sea, my body could tell if something was moving close.

The sound of clapping claws, opening and close, claws of death, in echoes in the wilderness. I couldn't see but my hearing was good.

Waist deep, I could feel tugging at my toes, snapping with the influence of popping them out of place.

My throat gave off an elephant cry, hurting my own ears. The moan of charley horses swimming in my toes, a spasm of working from the bottom to the top.

I grabbed for my left foot, to hopefully release the grip. The sock enclosing the pain, no such luck, the strain on the arch of my feet, curved and gave way. The hold, knocking my balance off.

SSPPLASH

As my face went under, air bubbles moving from under me to the surface. A wet base hand snatch at my face, I jumped up, putting pressure on my knees. I didn't know if I was east or west, from the shore, or north, south. My face coming up with a twist, I would be knee deep in the water with this push, if I was standing.

The sounds of crying in the wilderness, the echoes enchanted the crazy in me for survival. I know which way to go, follow the land noise, bringing in a funny smile to my face of, return of a Queen.

Losing myself in the background noise, kept my mind in movement, towards the noise.

As I stood up and proceeded, one of my feet finally hitting land, a chill came to the other one.

SSpplash

Falling on my knees, again, my foot got a drag back into the water. A tidal wave came to my waist. I could feel watery hands grabbing at my thighs.

I smacked at the water, it didn't change the channel of this flow coming to my calves.

Spplash

My hands clawing at the dirt within the liquid, to pull myself closer to shore.

It seems I was moving away from land. I got hit with a nasty tug to my ankles, smashing my face in the water.

Lights Off

Lights On

I pulled my face out, quickly, a watery image of me, staring.

I paused, trying to get it together.

Its hair was a red flame of fire, frowning, jello of liquid kool aid.

My fright snapped me into to a crawl to shore.

She was moving with me under the thin layer of water, frowning.

One of my hands out the water, touching down it would be hitting land.

She opens her watery mouth and closes it quickly, darkness.

A horrifying holler arose in the background.

My right hand connecting to land, as the other hand ready to do the same, a grab had it at the palms under the water. I tried to pull away but it was a little too late, the reflection was glued palm to palm with my left hand.

Her face grinning under me in the water, I begin to twist.

Sirens of converted quivers begin to ring in my ears.

An eclipse of this Amazon strength in H2O.

The ground and the ocean were moving together, as we wrestle, I wanted my hand back.

The reflection giving a smothering vibration of the ocean world.

In my left hand, the blood within it running in the wrong direction, starting a riot. Interception tainting me by the water levels within my knees.

The moon light gave emphases to the corroding of the reflection.

Everything happened in a split second.

Lifting my arms up, is if my strength was stronger then the weight of the world. My feelings of releasing from this liquid self portrait. A train of thought came in and settle with in my thoughts, "land", was better. Physically she had a weakness, air, and now we had to see who is stronger, me or I.

I started rolling toward land, viscously, not knowing the total gain.

Lights off

The rapidness of this move shut down all sight from the dizziness.

Lights on

In mid air, the ocean lying above me, as I laid flat on land.

The moon light not staying too much longer.

Staring, a rush of flavor filled my head, blood rising to the top, becoming the worst cream I could ever taste. The cream of confusion.

The reflection of her above, posing in the same position, several feet away.

A blue light coming threw the water.

A shadow of a shark fin upside down, showing it's where bouts, two feet away. This broke the staring trance of me and the deceiver I was seeing.

My arms were stiff; my control was of a stroke. Rehabilitation came to the muscle; a drop of water came down to my face, inspiration to the elbows, to sit up.

My volume was to stand up and ride this dream and swallow it whole. My palms twisted for a good push off the sand.

I had to get a grip first, my vision introducing a sea above, and land below. My eyes couldn't make out distance, how far long. I knew if I stood up, my head would be underwater.

I had to; my hands pushing up, rising up fast, but feelings was a mind blowing slowness.

I came closer to the water, so did she. She was jus as far as me from the border where water meets air. Mocking in a foolish follow the leader, as it seems to want to come out. The ocean hanging over me in the sky, breathing wouldn't exist with no air, if the water came crashing down. How would I survive? A grin appeared on the liquid reflection of me.

The top of my head touching the entrance to water, the roots getting a vindictive pull.

I won't be pulled in, she was getting pulled out. Ready!

My world, my rules, let's play, angrier having its way with me. Angrier of not waking up, I need to sleep with no more interruptions.

I put my hands in, hoping she would tag on.

She stuck to me, the reflection and I were coming together. I screamed, "The world is mine!"

My hand attached to hers, was lifeless, I couldn't feel a vein, tingle, or pulse, while a snapping sensation at the shoulder, felt like they was popping out of place.

I took the weight off my shoulder and let that side drop as my legs followed. My strength was greater than the weight of the world.

I plopped on my buttocks. This dead weight worked.

I could see the tip of a mirror finger coming out and went back in, the pointer. She was looking confused with spitefulness, her lips turning the color of blazing fire red within the water small waves.

I was pulling her to me, not I to her. She was furious.

She started changing glowing red, giving me a look of mistaken identity, of myself, her fraud showed and she and I were different. The reflection of a fool getting out smart.

My legs begin to slide in the wet sand. A plan in notion. The notion of keeping my faith, I would wake up and see the sun rise again.

I knew her weakness; she wanted me to think she had the power.

As I stared, sitting out on the sand, my arms holding my back support. I could see her body changing; her demeanor was stirring in confusion. I plan to reverse her soreness towards me.

The water moving away from me, she wasn't as intimidating, floating in my format above me.

I move my neck to view all of my surroundings again, her red glowing creating a hallway of red light reflection, shadows within the land at a distance.

Shadow of trees, not the root or branches, the middle. I couldn't tell which end was which. The branches or root were in my world are hers.

The planting of this wood was deep, either deep in the mud, hiding the limbs in the water or wading in the water with the branches spring on land. I wasn't sure because my eyes couldn't see that darkness.

I turn my head to a shadow, a shark fin. This water was low enough for it to come down and implant razor shape teeth in its choice, me or her. This land was not my opportunity it could be my fate.

I had to look up, she was seating exactly like me in the reflection. I could see the bottom of her watery feet reflection, sitting, palms close to the lining of water and air. The reflection of me looking up, from underneath me; retracted to the resemblances of the first mirror of my clones.

The bottom of her watery feet, stuck a real sharks stainless steel tooth.

Her world started transforming the curves and waves rocking, splashing salt water in my eyes.

Lights off

I jus wanted to wake up, no trauma, no distressed, no mass confusion, I wanted my wake up call, now.

Lights on

The shark body in the water was a dark shadow, growing with its movement.

The noise of claws clipping together, bold in a crazed perspective.

Splashes of water hitting my face, as I looked up.

She was staring, a watery reflection of red, her eyes were on fire.

I shrugged, now I knew this wasn't me at all.

She threw her hand at me quickly to get a grab in my environment. Hot boiling water hit my face and thighs. She had no grip in my world, air, her destroyer, even with this trial no win.

A shuffle with restraint, my eyes were closing, I had to put this out of sight out of mind, and my eyes need rest.

Lights off

A woozy cry enter my ears to pluck open my eyes.

Lights On

The jowls of life open up wide, underneath her. She was staring at me, full of rage. Her appearance of a jellyfish that was bright red.

The shark was not a shadow but real. It was coming from under her, vibrations felt in my feet.

The water showing a flow of adversaries in this culture, the shark wanted the reflection.

The shark grab, yank her down quickly, the tip of its nose coming out the water. Her movement of jellyfish caught in a wave.

She was staring mad; she never took her focus off me, as she went deeper. The clear watery image of her turning into a dark shadow, the presentation of a smog under water. The last of her dark light came with a splash of water hitting my face, more like a slap, the last of the dirty pool.

Lights Off

"Awake and ask", the thunderous voice heard in total darkness

Lights On

A blasted of blinding light. So bright it was tearing at the wetness with in them. Entering as a firecracker and exploding to cause a ricochet, as I stand still with my back on the sand. Natural causes of temporary shut down, a long held blink.

Lights Off

Chapter 8

That Dark Night

Lights On

I open to a startling sound, explosion. My sight was in tune, rumbling, as I lay, my face turned sideways. This lying was different, the brightness at the corner of my pillow, the bed shaking. I paused to make sure this wasn't a dream. The sounds of a bomb going off followed by another explosion, of a bright hot flare.

Lights Off

Lights On

I open my eyes; I was lying on my back in bed, a strawberry shortcake blanket, by my hands. A book opened, flat on my chest, Encyclopedia Brown.

"my Gershom", a familiar voice coming into the room.

The room space was little, a radio seating on a desk. The desk had a small book shelf on it. A couple of books for many topics; several of Nancy Drew and her mysteries. A Webster dictionary for understanding of words, threw my own eyes. Two, angel figurines standing tall, by the door, they were two feet tall. Two teddy bears, one on each of my night stands. The biggest prize won at the fair.

The two nightstands arranged between my bed one on each side. A vanity of fake jewelry, Mardi Gras beads, tossed on it. The small vanity sat opposite of the desk. Look toward the neon poster, my eyes made it back to the room door.

"Nighttime", as the voice made its entrance.

My mom was coming towards me, and kissed my lips. My lips were plucked and ready, for this attention from a love that was felt with the brightest smile.

The book closed and put on the floor by the nightstand, as I slide off the bed. Telling of thanks and giving recognition to the all.

Short but gratitude made, I climb back in the bed. "Amen", rolling off my mother tongue.

She pulled the covers to my shoulders and spoke, "the roses of flowers have glory, in and of GOD, my only daughter." One more kiss to the lips, as she proceeded to turn the lamp off, cracking the door as she left the room. The hallway giving enough light for reassurance that I was not totally in the dark. Listening I could hear the waves crashing with a hymn and splashes of humming.

My lids closed, I was happy everything was jus a bad dream. I was young and in my favorite room of all times. The present of my mother gave reassurance. I was ready for sleep and to wake up in the morning with a smile like no other.

Lights off

KABOOM!

A kick to my ear drums, of déjà vu, blades at war with my hearing. The terms of the root was tormenting my conscious of sound. Ringing coming in for a grand slam, sending tones of accompanied waves. Waves pointing to deeper waves, humming to insanity in my ears. Air with its own molecules of closure, taking in full endearment to the lungs. These sweet nothings were damage, to a state of mind. Sound came with full suspense. A sense was dieing, changing emotions to a fit of hearing shock. Trauma knocking and directing my interpretation of sound, to be, scared senseless.

Lights on

Startled my eyes open, flames out the door pouring into my room. My feet ready and hands started the fight, as fuzz took over sight.

An uncontrollable hotness taking over the back of my ears as I rose. My nostrils, in a figure four, being tackled by the scent. The smell, turning into a taste burning the back of my teeth, a nasty intake to the stomach.

I knew to run and get out.

"Momme-dadde. Heeelllpp", push out my stomach, choking my tongue. The cloud of red dark smoke, was tickling my tummy.

I got to my feet and ran to the window, not thinking of the performance on the other side of the door.

Opening the window came easy but the drop was another decoder. Slinging myself out the window was the reaction, with a childish thump.

Lights off

I laid, on the ground for a sec. The wind of air was knocked out of my lungs.

Lights on

My body lying on the ground, flat, I had to move. The fire coming out the bottom window and threw the down stairs wall.

Lifting myself up off the dirt, I could feel heat, hotter then the Sahara Desert, a heat wave moving closer. The activity of flames behind me, now scratching at my scalp, a sizzling coming to my hairs.

If the fire wasn't an instant torture, I would have taken my chance. Nothing could be seen in front of my sight, pure darkness. I didn't like the dark.

I could hear strong waves crashing at the seashore, and flocks of distorted wings in the air. This sound wasn't good to the ears, producing drops of blood to the drums. A luring rattle that came for its strike disturbing to my jaws. A pressure of locking came to the cheeks within, muscle of rude stitching.

"momme", rolled off quickly as my mouth felt the full reaction, this sound rang in my ears with a chill of deep echoes.

Limping forward, looking back sent a warm chill. Tall black flames moving toward me, covering the distance to the house. The roof produced its own horror.

Standing tall, a figure in a black robe, its height was at least eight feet tall. Robe waving with the smoke, unrealistic. A hood covered the head linking over the face. The face appeared to be its own shadow. The flames surrounding it as it stood in a mist.

Its arm stretched, the sleeve hung down a blurry darkness of a satin smoke blanket. Reviling a finger coming out, the pointer, at least six inches long. The finger of a skeleton, but shiny like red hot gold.

I thought, "What in the world," my temperature changing in my body. My feet in a sensation of being soaked in ice cubes, my brain was in another zone, it was place in boiling water and pulling out was no brain freeze. A third degree to the fifth power erupting.

I took off running, stepping on shells of a sharp kind. My blood was warm but the feet were still cold, the pressure of a pain.

My insight viewed slamming waves glowed once it landed, a little view of a boat tied to the pier.

I had to look back to see if someone had made it out and to view the image on the roof. A bon fire around my house as it stood in the middle of the blaze of dark flames. The finger curling up, three dimensional, in a suggestion of joining it.

The wall of flames moving to me, my skin started to feel the furnace.

Murmuring taking part in my hearing, the murmur of dieing wood, collapsing and falling apart.

I started to run, again, my body getting scared, influence, and gossiping about the surroundings.

Feet touching cold water, a world in front of me of darkness in a level of nature without humans.

Lungs pressuring the body to halt. The rudeness talked about among the veins, to reaction on its own. My veins slowed down and no action felt to the heart. Play time is over, shock was out of control.

The existence of lost and scared, embracing a minor was pretty risky business. In the mist, the howling to the note of hurtful terror.

Lights off

I had to catch my breathing; my oxygen level was becoming faintish.

Lights on

I was in isolation from the flames; I saw a robe growing over the house. The robe turning red as the fire, but darker. Its finger seems to be growing.

The sleeve moving towards me as if it was growing from the fire.

My pupils trying to get a grip on the hooded shadow of fire.

My senses knew to get to the boat. My feet enter the water as my socks became a sponge.

The boat tie to the end of a pole stuck in the water.

I could hear foot steps, behind me, marching to the pops of the flames.

I jumped inside, almost flipping the boat as I pulled at the rope. I was going to limit the space of the footsteps to no opportunity.

The little boat started to move to the waves, as I pushed off from the pole.

Looking hard with one glance within the small boat, a shadow coming in front of the boat, lying on top of the water.

Scared, I laid flat in the boat quickly, as I held onto the rope. The sky dark, with stars barely beaming threw.

A heavy drum sound coming in, a tapping came to my ears.

Moving my eyes round about, to movement down below my feet.

The noise getting louder in the darkness, while the waves were very terrible.

My hand reaches down and grabs a pair of old tennis shoes beating against the side of the boat.

I reached over to toss the shoes and peeking, the hooded thing was on the roof, arms seem to be folded.

I didn't need a splash so I placed them under my arm. No more peeking over the boat, this time I would lay until day light.

SPLASSSHHH

A big splash to my ears, the sound of a belly flop from a whale, I wouldn't look. Quietness came in for a pause.

Shaking with uncontrollable chills, echoes channel in.

My drums begin to ring, a moaning of help as it shut down.

Tears beginning to roll down my face in the shade of the stars, I stayed woke and eyes sewn open, many shadows worming around the stars. I laid still.

Sucking in the piercing scream of WHY!? WHY?!

Waves started to crash on the side of the boat, rocking me. Looking up the stars begins to fall; first one at a time, within minutes of the other, minutes turn to seconds. Falling fast taking away distance light until all had fallen.

I was falling asleep, coming to the nostrils and kissing the lungs good night.

Lights off

I knew this daily ritual would come into play. My lips moved to the thought of, "now I lay me, down to sleep, I pray the Lord my soul to keep, if I should die before I wake, I pray the Lord my soul to take, Amen."

I could feel my system shutting down as amnesia on the operating table. Exhausted was the conductor of the sleep….

Lights on

Rain drops falling on my face.

The sun giving a blindness of too much source, the drops were refreshing.

I glanced over the boat to bright shadows everywhere.

Ringing in my ears, strong and hard as I put my hands over them.

Panic kick in.

Lights off

I fainted.

CHAPTER 9
Stuck In A Stump

A sound of an over powering ringing came before sight, the new event of turbulence within my agriculture.

Welcoming me to the main withdrawal from sanity or insanity.

Lights On

Sunlight, beaming in my eyes, cooking the cornea to perfection, for appetite of success. I had to turn; my eyes came across, the view of a puzzle, mystery, or jail.

A wood box, I was inside another cage, a large tree trunk, filling removed. The spacing of the corners a 10 x 10, with four chairs facing each connection. I begin to get up.

The chairs were rusted and brittle, no seats or backs. The back of the chair look like handles, instead. The seats did have a picture frame in each. The frame, plain, four pieces of metal connect no picture or back. The chair seat width was a foot and the frame a foot and a half, equally hanging off the side. The bottom of the frame, slid to the back of the seat, the top lean on the wall. My curiosity was of escape which was inconclusive. An opening to exit was now the quest as the tone of bells ringing getting lower. I took my hands off my ears and started a turn of my environment.

My appearance was normal of a grown woman but my shoes were gone, the right hand still wrapped up. No pain jus dried up blood. The dirt was under my feet and wood was the walls of confinement, I took a step closer to one of the chairs scenery, to view one of the replicas.

One step

The chairs begin to rock side to side. The frame sliding on the chair making a long violin noise.

Step two

Within arms reach the chair started hit both sides of the wall.

I glanced up, a journey of the mind, lost within a small box; the sun shine was to strong, blistering with a nimble at my flesh. I notice the height of the walls, one story up. The sun sending sensation of burning without control. The heat waves numbing at dehydration, felt at the finger tips, my toes fumbling as it tries to resist, the hot ground.

Noise hitting the air waves of glass breaking in high definition to the muscle in my neck. The root jumping to a beat in the jowl bone, the roots within my channels.

Sharp and damaging to the ear drums which was in need of plenty tender loving care.

Lights off

Not again, enter my conscious, not again.

Lights on

The noise of the glass breaking, hurting to the ears, which cause a strain closure to the eyes.

The tree carvings were different each side, but the glass fallings were all the same. Every piece in the same spot in each area. The breakage wasn't many pieces, but a few, maybe seven or eight. It looks as if the piece fell out the picture frame?

The chairs still moving rapidly, causing a stomp on the ground that made the glass started to bounce up off the sand.

The chatting of solid drums from an African warrior, coming to terms with stampeding horses holding great armor. The war between thunder and an earthquake, it could only be felt. Lightening being their boiling point of explosion, seeing and feeling its power. The sun was the lightening with no break, touching the top of my head, hot to effect it was closing in, a ceiling without a roof.

I realized a trap, I knew how rules apply, so many rules of convincing the manual of my mind that I ain't right, in more ways than one. My order was to wake up, and find a memorial of sanity.

Keeping my movement at a stop, to observe, nervousness of release came from the thumbs while the fingers keep a certain control. My nerves jumping, I was tired of this mind game. I had to stop it, so I could live my life, normal.

An idea hit my temples with a roaring crash, creating a migraine. "Get to the root of the problem," squeezing my pressure point as the thought enter.

I ran the three steps to the middle of one of the wood walls, between two of the chairs. I dropped down and begin to dig.

The coarse of the sand was breaking my nails with ease.

The chairs vibration is moving violently and the ground throwing everything off balance; chairs, glass, frames, and including me.

A change of events, I was now knocked on my side. A flame from the sand, that brought me to my feet. That spot felt like the hottest spot on earth, to my legs and arms, other spots were raging, not this one it was heat activated for a cremation burial.

A strong laughter of shame, song in my ear, coming from every angle, my eyes turned. On the jumping ground the broken glass, were mirrors. The mirrors had my red lips in each pieces, shading around them was dark.

As clear as the sun, it started to rain, the sky producing a sizzle to the refreshment of the liquid introduction. I knew the sun never stops burning even in the mist of storm.

The fluid hitting my face in a force of steamy con screwed justice. The flow hurting the bruise skin with a luxury, turning into a different source conning, trickery of the weather.

The mirrors sinking into the quickening mud, the chairs being included as it stop its temper tamper.

An escape plan aroused as my feet begin to sink. "Get to the root," optimistic is now the liberty bell, shaking me into think mode.

As the rain stop, the ground was cool enough to start this process.

The digging was wrong; water started seeping in from the hole I was digging. It was no way out, my face turning red, as I jerked my neck, slapping me back to focus.

The flow coming in with a pace of strategy, this stump was based around water.

Laughter pick up strongly in the background, strongly by the sinking mirrors.

My survival was at state, and surviving a tide while rearranging my steps.

I knew it wasn't a waiting period, time for the action.

I looked over to my right, uneven ground, the chair half way in the mud puddle in the corner. "think," spring up within my mind.

I looking at the other three remaining, tilted on the wall, I got an idea.

This is uneven ground; those chairs not yet sunk in mud, jus the one.

I rushed and grabbed one chair and run to the other one, away from the stream coming in.

The grab turn into a serious choke hold, thorns in the chair. The rust was dried up vine of thorns, which grew around it, cutting and sticking to my hand. A mouse trap full with extras, extra pain making extra strength that could only be within. The push of satisfaction of that moment of escape.

I made way to the corner, holding on to the chair for dear life, until-quickly. Picking up the other chair and placing this chair upside down on top of the other. The release of the chairs was joy and I knew I only had one try or I would have no more, the chair position wouldn't be stable in the mud. Building an escape to resurface, my instinct kicking in, no matter what I had to find a way, OUT!

No water at the top, so I had to go for it.

The pool close to my heels, I put my hands on the tree and step up to a balance of sharp angles gnawing at the bottom of my feet. I had to balance with patience, certain muscles had to corporate, because if it didn't I would tip over.

I start the climb.

The crunch of brittle dried up stems, the feeling to me as if they weren't dead.

My last leg off the ground, and the feeling of pressure to my ankles.

I look down and the thorns were growing vines, forming around my ankles.

I didn't care any more about the pain my body built up some tolerance. The suffering of a obnoxious jail.

My arms taking the weight as I balanced to my next act.

This chair was trickery, facing the wall ready to break. The challenge my weight and its holding power of a rusty chair.

I slid my hands slowly on the wooden wall, pulling the vines with me, palms flat.

The vines snapped and the balance was made easier. Easier doesn't mean, no more obstacle in the future, jus a breath in between.

The sun rays bright and the relief of the rain, was gone.

If I stood straight, that would put my hands on the edge.

Intruding the sounds of slamming waves on the other side. A vibration around the tree shook the chairs and water raced rapidly from the hole, I dug, and coming close to underneath the chair I'm on.

The imbalance of balancing, flexing with weak stamina, humming with integrity. The fractions equal up to, keeping my balance and making myself as light as a feather. The hold was the forceful neighboring pain. My body was starting to shake; I had to control my panic attack.

It put a crook in my persuasion of constant hurtful moments to survival.

I peek down and the chair was sinking in the black mud. The river of darkness mixing with flammable sand.

My fingers grab the edge; a shadow flies over my head.

The chair getting a touch from the rising mud. I knew it was going to collapse, my legs push off.

Sounds in the air of flocking crows, chatting about a feast.

One of my legs thrown over, making a balance of my body straight down the middle of measurements of the width, six or seven inches. The snap of my joints in my calf was crucial to my intelligence, to release a hold of bondage to the frontal lobe.

My grip on both sides of the trees shifted a leveling of a scale of gravity of both sides of my body.

I looked down and the chairs were broken on the muddy ground, fading fast as the water rose. The mud creating the feel of no way out within the trunk, a sinking of a wave of sand that over power the flow of water.

My body leveling on my stomach, now lying on the top of the stump, I started peering at my surroundings. I could see trees everywhere on these islands.

The roots of all, under water, the scene of a hidden forest. The where bouts in this areas, of no understanding.

I could see a dark flame underneath some trees, even submerged in water.

Others were many eagles in some of the trees that were burnt to a crisp, no fire within the brittle limbs. Others totally on fire with no notice of smoke, jus a red flame.

I looked down a long drop off the stump. It was a couple of strokes in this country of water to the next island with a tree and the next and the next. The Greenland, with the view of forestry in a disaster zone. I had a ten foot drop into the mud surrounding this part of the trunk.

The sun making me queasy, I want to get shade and nurturing of any kind.

The stump I was laying on was the only stump, no branches or top, but solid.

Trying to look behind me, I accidentally slide off.

Boooooom

I hit the ground not the mud to hard.

Lights off

CHAPTER 10

The Wake Up

"Read it," *the voice said* sternly.

My mind begins to wonder in this hypnotizing voice, of my past occurrences. I was preparing myself. Rewinding back to the haunting past.

Laughter…

Lights off

Splashhhh

Lights ON

The water was cold.

The water cleared out my ears of demonic laughter in echoes of bouncing sound.

Water filling my lungs, I was panicking in the water.

A hold on my thighs, as I slap the surface for air.

It released, as my face surface.

I could see shadows of creatures on all fours, hollowing to a beat of crazed beasts.

Yanked underwater at the knees by the shadow, I kicked and pushed off the shadow, it was a solid form.

Doggie paddling forward to the red light sounds attacking my ears in the water.

The shadow claws coming at me again. I kicked harder.

Yanked under again, looking into the water green eyes, I could feel bubbles, as I pushed off harder.

This push it took its grip off, franticly.

I looked forward and the creatures at the shoreline, front legs splash in the water. The dark red shadows of four legged creatures, four of them.

My state was in shock, my reverse to face the real. The crabby shadow underneath in this liquid of torture was a boy. I was kicking him in the face as I pushed off.

My swimming out of control, I could see the wolves' shadows, change before I went under. They were other boys cheering him on, the sounds of a pack of hungry wolves smacking at the water.

I was in shock, as I went under, reviling the brightness wasn't the sun but the chlorine burning my eyes.

Lighting off.

Reversing my thoughts to Lights on, I laid flat beside the pool, the roof was covered with the look of an aquarium. The look would bring a cooling to my soul. The waves of water gave me a good sleep, remembering a time by the beach, comforting. I heard noise as I slept, I sat up, still hadn't woken fully up. A surprising drag in the pool, a joke from a joker. The riddle was not to see or hear but torment my character.

They had turned off the lights once they saw me lying there, to give a lustful hunt to their game. They were hype up from football practice. In the bodies of grown men but the minds of immature fools. Their course was a dare of influence to make a trick of an innocent bystander. Sliding me in the pool with the practical joker that want acceptance.

The teal light being my glow in the dark watch which wasn't water proof.

They forgot about the red light that always came on at the deep end of the pool, for safety precaution.

My moment towards the light changed the wolves' movements. They ran to that side, to give off the biggest fuss, to my chase from their friend. They were ready for the consequences of either the crab under me, are the take on of four of them. They started splashing the water with their hands, anxious for the ending.

The wolves yell in the splashes of the water, as I fought the water with no restrictions.

A dark shadow coming close underneath me, I was fully clothed.

My thoughts travel quickly, to the shadow underneath me. I kick him so hard that it choke him. His fight was to retreat. My mind still asleep but in a state of awareness.

My ears rung to the pressure of, "Evil, STOP IT!!! She's drowning!!!"

Deborah jumps in the water enraged by what she walked into, right over the red light.

The missing of her bus, turn into a three hour wait on her ride. So she decided to read by the pool, until her pick up. She chose to wait which turn into a moment of tribulation for time.

She swims to me, my eyes close to a dead man float. Deborah yelling in the water, "I ain't scared of you fuckers. She can't play but I'm ready to dance!" "Cutting is my tango!!"

The scattering of fools caught on camera, towards the exits.

She reach me and begin to pull me out the pool, everybody else was gone.

This riddle solved, I was certified as life guard, not drowning but half sleep. The best riddle solved, on how this friendship became even stronger.

Covers being yank from my face.

A teenager face, right in front of my face, "Get up! Read my lips Get Up!" a grin from Deborah. My lips frown, not finding a thing funny.

"Boo who, sun is out, and its time to eat," Deborah spitted in my face as she spoke.

I mugged her face back, smiling she put her hand in the air and stuffed half a biscuit down her mouth, with little measures of chewing.

I smiled and blew up my cheeks, she was being over hyper to the taste or either very hungry.

Rising her hand to her mouth, to present an invisible cup of drink, opening her mouth, full of biscuit and sticking out her tongue. Deborah jotted out the door to retrieve moister to the mouth.

Lifting my legs out the bed letting the ray of sun, touch my temple. A welcome glancing I gave as I looked out the window.

A tear rolled down my face as I looked out the window. "Thank You", my lips read.

These humble thanks to GOD, churning my thoughts, to fill it with knowledge, and understanding, in a shade of wisdom, I survived. I knew I was a little angry of the situation that occurred; this would pump at my nerves later. Of a destruction that was building, I should have giving it up but the mind was covering it up to show in my later reaction to men. The way of the world would weigh me down if I didn't let it go. The ending of the closure of this angrier would be my beginning to stop self destruction, only time would tell me the clues of releasing with a positive flow.

I closed my eyes to the thoughts of good, bad, and the ugly.

I jump into my flutter of thoughts, to wishing on a falling star.

The wish of always being comforted by my mother.

As I open my eyes to barely catching the last flick of fallen star, I could see next to the window something staring. The clock of an owl, but the eyes had a glare of other eyes. These eyes, in a haze, were mingling with rage.

The Dragon!

I closed my eyes to remember the wish.

Open my eyes to a tunnel, at the end of it a light turn on.

Remembering the falling star, I open my thoughts.

My feet step into wetness, this set off a bell.

Shoes on my feet, the fashion of Nike's, smooth with lights at the bottom. These shoes were made for joggers or night walkers, too expensive and childish for a middle schooler.

Instant replay of the real enters the mind being shocked in and out of conscious.

I was sleepwalking, not because of my own reaction, but by force.

Self consciously the mind wanted to wake up, to examine abuse in the full effect, the butterfly effect.

My reversal of my thoughts, the lights turn off as my shoes begin to shine.

My shoes begin to get wet, as I focus in thought. My feet were in a small clear pool of water.

My eyes reviled I had on my day clothes.

A brush to the hair and breathing down the back of my neck, the sounds of whispering and sniggering, filled the room.

I froze

The eyes of the dragon glowing in the dark right before my face, the next I felt myself falling backwards.

The balance made me lay flat on my back.

She was tainting me, showing me she's the biggest. Her friends were in the other room laughing and talking bad about her cooking. She felt the need to produce her own bully to someone else to relief her pain with a dash.

I stepped into the pool of water, unconsciously; my mind was trying to wake up. My body produced a dead weight to her tug. She gave me a cold push to maintain her dominance. She pushed my head, and this landed me flat on my back.

She steps back and closes the shower curtain. She left the bathroom, cracking the door behind her, satisfied. The tub was a foot deep of cold water.

Doesn't my step mother know, that I'm not fully woke, the reason for the pause, semi shock to be forced to sleep and walk. In her craziness she had place me right under the faucet which was still dripping.

The bang to the head keeps me in sleep mode. The shoes giving off a shine that was letting me see the undiscovered. My shoes giving the tub, a cave of lighting.

The shoes a gift from her, to show that she spent money on me, but she knew it was embarrassing for my age.

I was moving wildly, my mind is still half sleep, trauma to the head put me deep in. My body sliding back and forth, in a earthworm fashion.

The cellular phone was going dead on the counter, two red lights to show, one going dead and someone still on the line. In the phone sound waves were heard, "Bitch, take a bath, you're not a young lady, you're a filthy bum."

Her abusive but unusual punishments, to making me take a bath with reasoning. She waited until sleep was deep, to enter my room and yank me from my bed.

Not realizing I'm tired from having a full day; I laid across the bed for only a minute and end up falling asleep.

The height of water was filling up my lungs. The shower head still dipping water, splashing in my face. The water level was rising while I couldn't evaluate the scene.

One of the females visiting went the wrong left, and made a right. She was walking and talking, with a grin, reading of the lips read, "you can't cook, no sugar coating it, I need some water."

She paused in the hallway were she heard splashing. She decides to take a peek at the commotion. She cracked the door, wondering if Flaky the cat was tearing up in there.

She whispered, "What is going on in the bathroom at this time of night."

She peeks in, and my shadow was on the ceiling. I was lying on my back as my arms and legs swaying.

"My bad," rolled off her tongue, thinking dang she's having fun.

No fun, I was slowly drowning, a seizure was at hand from the shove.

Ira, stop in her tracks, "girls that age, don't play in water like that", murmured off her lips.

She turns around in her tracks, and knocked lightly on the door.

"Gershom, you in here," as she slowly open the door, realizing the light switch would be better. Ira put her hand in the door and moved the switched up and down, twice.

The splashing got softer, but no answer or peek out of the shower curtains.

She rushed over and instinct kicked in. She pulled the curtains back to a fully clothed female.

This is what she saw in a flash.

I was on my back. The water dipping but my face underwater, except for most of the nose. The nostrils had the best of both worlds half in or half out. My skin was pale and face was blue but life was still in me.

She yanked me out of the bathtub and started the Heimlich maneuver. Ira was trying to keep her balance on the wet floor, slipping and sliding. She never dropped me, holding on to me for dear life.

The females in the front room giggle heard.

"HELP!!" rung off Ira's tongue, as she struggle to keep her feet planted.

Life given back.

After that night the red eyes of the dragon were gone. The dragon name was Molly. She was so pretty and intelligent but her looks were so deceiving, full within of ugliness. The red eyes showed it, a profane dragon glowing in my thoughts.

I open my eyes to a different kind of red eyes, staring. Blinking hard, I open wide to a whip flew over my head in the air as I was looking up toward the ceiling.

The room moving in and out.

The blobby shadow moving and the sound of rope lassoing in the air, ready for action. The strange laughter spread in the background.

The figure of a shadow on the wall, big and round.

I look towards the sliding doors in this room. I could tell the city was alive and well, over the balcony. This room worth thousands per night, a invitation to wealth of worldly kind.

The beeping of horns, the pacing of the engines, talking of conversations of none of my concern, walking with steps amongst many, heard loudly. I could hear too much, rattling in my ears, the wrong sound colliding together.

I looked toward the mirror stand, and flashes of men faces with the wrong kind of smile coming in fast right behind the other, so many. I had to close my eyes.

As one came forward it pushes the other out, creating a flipping album of horny little devils in a portfolio.

The faces of my payers, to take them away from their problems, with a lust full of appeal. The faces setting off a new trend, channeling the stress from work, spouses, children or their real lives. It's retaking of abomination of the lustful kind. The sin from a money inspired whore of a beautiful kind among filthier minds.

This slender payer in the room, paid good, so money was needed. He saw his self as the fattest when actual he was closer to being the smallest. His angrier with food created a danger of self mutilation, until he let me have the job.

The job, and the only way I could deal with it, was the man made stress relievers, drugs and alcohol would get the mind off focus. I grin at the thought his bruises would tell on me, without knowing, who **I** am. He carved the whip and enjoyed getting beat. My secrets it was time to be face, to change my enter face to see reality. To save myself, from myself, the ugly shame.

Once he walks out the room, time to get away from everything, more pills raced down my throat, a monster I created. I fell in a daydream under high dosage, which brought on a sleepwalking of a fantasy zone. The beginning of the learning that I was my worst enemy, chasing a dream of riches. The glutton of it presented in my grin, easy as turning on the Lights. The light of who was I at this time?

Running outside the room full Monte, I peeked back in. My sight ready to be influenced by a high that was pass floating. The monster was creating its own mind over matter. My feet in tar, not, my feet feeling the effects of alcohol poisoning.

Look back in my sanity play with my conscious, seeing my dangerous life. Who was Gershom, me, myself or I? This a deadly meeting place, inside a delusional mind.

A mirror place directly in front of the door, as I looked in it. I was controlling the show, the image showing the confusion of this sinner. The bad girl gone wild, the wrong phrase to be in, a smirk in the mirror.

The gripping of my clothes and purse, as I enter back into the hall to get dress. The movement from the other whores' could be heard in the hallway and all their snakes. This hotel in the stock market, represented as the most fabulous.

The peeper in one of the rooms, entertain by listening, saw that I was in the hallway along. Press up against the peep hole, observing.

Over paranormal, making sounds out my throat as I ran to the elevator. As I ran moaning in the hallway, lusters finally came out the rooms. The over screaming, saved my life, the sneaky peeper got scared of being caught. The doors open up to declare witnesses, if I came up missing.

The elevator open, I didn't realize I was scaring a passenger in the mist. The passenger asked, "Are you alright." Of course I didn't hear, bringing her hand to tap me. I gave a huge yank, the female step back in the corner. She looked at my face, covered with sweat and redness, with a wideness of insanity taking its toll on my eyes. Her eye contact cause a reaction to me swinging my arms to get her eyes off me.

I exit the elevator doors with a shove from my conscious. The sounds of earth and people enter into my ear drums. I made it to the street, as vision came in blurry.

I Fainted in a overdose state.

I could hear, "momme", the voice of a boy enter my head.

The paramedic was waving his hands in my face while placing something under my nose. Didn't work I went totally out.

I realize that I need help, in some shape, form, or fashion.

I was seating in the waiting room of the psychologist office. My head face the ground, and I felt a burning in my face.

I looked up and the little girl's face in my face. Her eyes grabbed hold of mines. The stare was burning my vision.

Her eyes round like pearls, but the color of amber.

She stared even though her body was going a different way.

I closed my eyes. I knew seeing a shrink would help with getting a new leaf on life.

The real surprise was sitting in the waiting room.

She hypnotized me in her office minutes earlier; she carried the title of the best of the best of Psychiatrist. The Chief of Liaison psychiatry was the name of her top seller's book.

My mind still stuck on, releasing my sin, within my sleep. Snapping her fingers to open my eyes, she didn't know- it took more to fully wake me up, I was a sleep walker. Sleep walkers walk with their eyes open.

Drifting in my thoughts as I sat in the waiting room, awaiting my ride. The little girl staring at me, as I stood up and proceeded to follow them out the doors. She held on to her grandma's hand to lend the way, while she stares, keeping the eye in contact.

I could hear, "you are not alone." This voice was harmonizing within harps. The little girl eyes, locked on mine. She jus stared not of fright but she could hear, too. The moment those words were heard the little girl, could hear the sound. The words rolling out my mouth, no movement of the lips, "always there."

I was talking within my sleep, and she understood even when no one else could hear. My spirit was trying to comfort me to understanding.

Her grandmother saw the stare and quickly grabs the little girl, rushing out the door.

The little girl repeated to the grandmother, "no estás solo?"

The girl replied, "siempre hay," as her eyes came forward. She had bump into a lady with a baby stroller, going out the door first.

The grandmother gave a look of concern as she looked at her granddaughter and pulled her in front of her.

"disculpanos," came from the grandmother as they made it out the doors.

I was still in a trance; the waiting area was the rude unwavering awake. The thoughts in my mind to give sympathy to a stubborn mind.

Innocence was in the room, the little girl could hear clearly. She was the break in my sleep and waking up; I had to talk to her in a room full of moment.

The rain starting coming as I walked to the door, it was automatic sliding door. I step out to freezing cold. I froze, looking into the watery doors; as they closed. I could see what happen, minutes before my exit, a déjà vu reversed.

In the watery vision, the little girl seating, she looks toward the glass doors, as the rain poured down. My seat was unseen from this area.

(I recollected my thoughts, thinking did the Doctor of Osteopathic Medicine not know. I was taking in the notion of our conversation. My sins, my conscious, my lost for self worth, a rose is still a rose; now it was on my mind in a different kind of roar.)

The pedestrians worry about not getting wet to notice a female staring at the doors, as she stood in the rain.

I was stuck in my own illusion, the coming to grips of a clever kind.

I press up against the glass door to go back inside, which was an exit, the entrance door was right next to it. The entrance door came open. My mind didn't realize it was letting me in, out the rain, but I couldn't move any where but down.

The vision of ghostly shark fin in the watery scene in front of me, posing in the rain drops, and faded away.

I drop down, into a tired sleep.

Hypnosis, pain killers, and gin and juice, wasn't profitable to a sleep walker.

The little girl turns right at the end of the building under her grandma umbrella, in my direction. The sounds of trumpets took over her eardrum; it was louder then a horn. She screamed at the top of her lungs as she covered her ears.

Her grandmother thought it was the thunder that scared her, and pick her up and ran to the right, out of sight.

Chaim was her name; this little girl has a precious gift of an even deeper hearing, emphases of this would show in the next manuscript.

This noise alarmed the security guard to investigate the sound coming from the open door.

The rescue of a Good Samaritan paying attention to his job, rain or shine.

I was being pulled into the building by strong force of hands.

The scream was too much to my sleepy mind.

I went into deep sleep, a coma.

This would be the inbox that would let my thoughts come in for a shot. The shot of redemption.

The monster, the drugs moving out my system, as I laid in my bed, in a trance while I look into my dresser mirror to the side of me.

Facing me, facing my sins, I would fight this time no surrendering to a nothing cause.

The first project to see myself as the beautiful ugliness of a crying whore. The facing of my demons so they could flee, resentment and rebuking of it so it would never return. The start of long journey of freedom, the shattering of layers of nasty coats of destruction, one step at a time.

I stood up and cracked the mirror with my fist, no shattering or noise to let it be known. My disgust by my appearance of ignorance, blood dipped from my hand. I hit the mirror again to produce a chill to my hand. The mirror cracked, but didn't break; damage to my hand was doubling.

The sunlight coming from the sun roof was leaving, as my reconstruction of seeing my sins proceeded.

The sun was a gift, not treasured like it should be. Until this day, the need of the light was shown to keep sight. The light always in front my face even through the reflection lies. Time to make that first step to change, to master that woman in the mirror, threw the grace of GOD.

The swirling of my emotions, the drug and alcohol infested monster; my weakness, one was the receiving of money and showing the tricks of the snake. The snake, my payers the root of lustful sin, an introduction to face this insanity and to conquer and destroy.

The second weakness letting go of my abuse, from the chair, a fear of control. I would handle it by forgiving and then it could be used as a helper, later.

Ready to break the cycle of a curse, the time of escape, and a challenge of coming to grips.

The shattering of layers of nasty coats of destruction, one step at a time.

The shattering of the window with a chair, in my room, as a disturbing knock came to my door. The door is locked with another chair, seen in the mirror behind me, for protection in my sleep. The sun was now at the window, ready to set. They didn't know I was a different kind of sleep walker, original, undeniable I was different, a class of its own.

I climb out the window with a mummy state to my movement. The area outside woody, and a man built waterfall, ahead, at the top of this hill. I knew within, home was where the heart is, my childhood home was on the other side of a waterfall.

In a quick thought, I could see myself looking out my window as a child, looking at the waves under the stars.

I move faster to the waterfall, my instinct was to pick up a stick even in my thoughts of sleep, for protection. Thinking, thinking, the dragon, if she gets near me, I would fight. I begin to realize what angrier, Molly had cause.

I started to run to the waterfall. I embraced the thought of my son, Benjamin the cancer, over the mist of hungry wolves in my life. The fight within my thoughts of happy over sad, the meaning my son love was more powerful then the terror that remain within a scared female of a past haunting. He always loves his mom even when I forgot about him on my addiction filled days.

I still couldn't wake up; I made it to the lake, rushing to get over the waterfall. A boulder sat in the middle of the fall give enough room to stand on. I got on it.

My mind went into a shock in my sleep, coldness of the water, and a chill coming out of it. My face of a zombie, the medicine, giving a deep sleep with an enhancing shift of walk it off.

Chasing the light in the middle of a nightmare, my weaknesses were present to give off a scale.

I looked down and saw a shark fin, in the waist high water. I started climbing the side of the waterfall. The night noises started coming in, rough.

My sins trying to bring me down, coming into to play for its last straw. My exaggeration saw the same, highly doped up, the whip was the snake. The real action a dead tree limb in my path up, I begin to hit the branch with the stick, both dropping into the water below.

I looked down and the shadow of a shark. I start back climbing the waterfall. The sun was almost gone on the other side of the hill. The shark shadow moving and waiting a dark creature on its back, standing. A dark black velvet robe was its clothing, the hood looking down, not a glance up. The shark shadow disappeared as the robe spread, covering the entire top layer at the bottom of the fall. The hood robe was unknown of the character underneath, but I knew, the same one pointing its finger with a twirl. Melting with the water, change it's appeal of watery robe, not flame. A hurl in the air, the shark as it rapture threw the robe coming straight towards me, the big black snake in its mouth. It lands back in the water with no splash.

Death would come to all, even snakes.

My focus came back up to my surface, I was on top of the cliff. I look right into, red eyes, waiting for me to look into them.

My delusion was normal as the doctor say, something to take off the edge. My thoughts mixing back to hearing the voice of Chaim, she would become a great teacher.

A wave came in with a charm, the attention getter, to get some revelations.

My body getting weak from the prescription that was digesting. I felt sleeper and lonely in this wilderness, this time I always remember, ask, and time to pray.

My deepest thought came in for my Faith, "yea, though I walk through the shadow of," water hitting my face.

"death, I will fear no evil," water coming in my nose, the lake had its own undertows, waiting for the right step.

"for thou art with me," my face getting dashed by the wave.

I open my eyes to a wave hovering over my head. The scene in the actual format, I was in the lake flopping like a fish, sleep taking on a new wave. I was tripping within a mirage of myself, my dosage cause a fight within. My thoughts knew I had to brake free from my sins, even in a delusion. The sins of I, weren't ready for none of this, no repenting, it wanted its control.

I was worthy of a new wave, a new beginning, I had to let it go.

The push back to life, I was getting strength for my life while in sleep.

The seahorse the favorite sea creature of my mother, she loves to sing and she knew I love the water.

Strength can't come to sin if sin can't be used. I was in a coma, my lust couldn't win in a dream. The more I laid the weaker the physical sin became.

The whore angry of the outcome of my decision for wisdom, having its last shuffle of seduction to control me. Its leadership couldn't control without the fear, of my past.

The beats of my heart changing to the pattern of lights off and On with charley horses coming in the race, shutting me out of reality, an overdose of an crazed outbreak of my character.

I realize she had no control over me, no consideration of my willing being. As long as I was breathing I had a second chance, air, her destroyer. I was realizing I could get a second wind.

The shark wanting parts of this rapture.

The shark?

The shark giving me a jump in thoughts.

I could see shadow of a lady walking towards me. I was in bed.

Kaabboom!!!

The ringing made an automatic closure of my eyes.

Opening them the shadow of a lady exiting the room.

Kaabbooomm!!

This cause a quick startle, that shook off quick.

Flames racing in the room, I ran to the window, sleep was still waving the air. The shock of the rude awaken, sparks in the brain.

Heeelllp", rolling off my tongue.

As I got up from the fall that knocked the wind out of me, "Mommie," rolled off my tongue. A word that could be my last.

I looked back and the smoke making a hooded figure on the roof top.

Fast forward in the boat, peering to the side I could see it, the hood creature burning on the roof top.

The boat floated into the sea, darkness surround my eye lids until the tears in my eyes put me to sleep.

I knew death had placed itself in my home. I didn't know of the outcome. I did know I was still breathing.

As the sun touched my face in a blurry heat. One of the members from the search team, sees the boat, and starts swimming into the water, for me. This created a running in the water from many for the hopes of my safety. The swimmer splashing into the water to race to me, I could feel the drops hitting my face. This woke me to a half sleep; I looked over the boat to be place with bright shadows.

I had made it to the other side of the lake, with a ringing in my ear.

To much, I fainted.

I knew, later the hooded shadow, got one victim in my home. The explosion of gas water heater, the cause of my mother passing and took chunks out of me.

My mind flipping on the tree the last voyage to understanding, to face the truth.

I had to find away out of misery and letting it stay behind. The way out was hard and painful, but rejoicing my stump could have been on fire. I had to let go and not worry about my surroundings but get an escape, even if it means trying more then one way. Finally got the right one. Taking my haunting past and using them to help me, giving my debtors a forgiving fate, as they can pay it forward to next neighbor.

I was reborn within my deep sleep.

I close my eyes to shake off my sleep.

As my eye lids open, the mouth of a shark in front of me. I closed my eyes.

"gggeerrsshhom", a distance voice of a female.

"mommie," rolled off my tongue.

"WAKE UP", a stern male voice enters my ear with force. "Since you can't see me, then hear Me!"

The motion of the time of me getting to the waterfall and now was created in flashes and withdrawal, my mind was getting right.

I open my eyes to darkness, sound came to a still. A blurry vision coming into picture, of hands waving.

Lights off

"Hear", the strong voice of the wind, planted deep within the ear sockets.

Lights on

Blurriness of a dull light filled my face.

"The Truth", I heard in the wind as it quickly faded out.

A shark opens mouth, blinking in and out of my sight.

I open my eyes a figure sitting on my bed, my hands under my head of a little girl, my eyes focused clear. My daddy sitting on the side of the bed, his neck covered with a tattoo of the open mouth of a shark He's words, "are you not my daughter, I changed because of you." "I use to conquer the seas in cave diving," as he pointed to his tattoo covering his neck and back. "Razeil, the bull nose shark," with a manly chuckle. "Finding hidden treasure of many riches, but the treasure wasn't the hunt it was you. Close caption of malfunction to my mouth piece, let me see gluttony of money, wasn't the search. You got to want the better change, of Peace. The search for true existence, what it is, what it was, and what's its always going to be." "I find out love conquers all."

My eyes ready to blink, I closed with a smile.

To the splash that was heard outside the boat, my father was trying to see if I had got out and was hiding, but my shock couldn't hear his screaming. The boat drifting rapidly in the waves, his lungs full of smoke stopped his swim.

I open slowly, making sure not to change my thoughts.

My dad was here for me the whole time, reading the Bible, and talking to me in my coma. I finally heard him with the help of past rewind, it had been a long time, and I kept myself deaf to his preaches, for years. He knew my path; he once was on the same road of destruction.

The drugs moving out my system was causing me to get a grip on breaking my sleep. The release of sleeping off my sins. The illusion of my mind and heart, breaking the cycle, in a way of untouchable matters of the soul.

I closed my eyes, inhaling with a smile.

CHAPTER 11

What Seek Ye?

Lights On

Strong male voice, cloudy as it spoke, "Dear John, questioning signs of the times and wonders of miracles."

Darkness surrounded shadows on the wall, hands moving rapidly.

"Can forty eight go into four?"

The hands fell to the side hard and a bright light came into my eyes "Read it, John 4, verse 48."

My eyes open wide to young man on the stage with a microphone. He pulls his face closer to the standing microphone. I looked right at his lips, "The Believer, My Mother, The Dreamer, and the Speaker."

I got out of my chair and processed to the stage.

As he turns, his hands cuffing his lips around the microphone.

His words whispering in the microphone, "I hope she keeps her eyes clear of tears, because I won't, this speech wasn't practice, straight from the heart."

As he placed his hands back to his sides, he walks to meet me, with a kiss; I could see a big smile.

As I walked up to the microphone, "Giving all honors to GOD." "my only son, Benjamin", (turns and looks toward her son, sitting in the crowd of dimness). "The reasoning for permanent change, to the opening of my eyes and ears." "Libbi the gift which gave more power to the change." A teenage girl smiling next to Benjamin, a spot light shining on the both of them.

The spot light shining back above my head.

Libbi knew her birth was a gift to her mother.

79

"Even though this is the first time speaking in public. This speech is in my heart, paper nor pen would do it justice. As I sat here, I relived my negatives tribulations in thought, to produce a positive of my trials in this speech. Even though I can't hear my words, my voice was never taken away. A testimony of hearing with new ears, the under coating."

"To all that don't know, I'm deaf, I lost my hearing in the explosion, and if I couldn't hear my own voice, why speak. I'm up here letting you know, I'm living proof, the Son of GOD is our servant, and the begotten Son is the reasoning. My hearing is gone but all of you can hear my speech clearly. I decide to speak because I have to save one. I realize some time ago that my self pity was pulling me away from GOD. The worst pity."

"This was my obstacle illusion.

One: I lost my mom, home and hearing in the same day, so I thought I had means for my sorrows.

Two: Two years later, I was introduced to an abusive step mother, in the sneakiest ways. A chair was one of the constant punishments to show her angrier and to introduce another weakness to being, bullied. I would sit several hours facing the wall, one of her reasoning for confinement was an unannounced burp that came out my mouth as she and I sat at the dinner table. Other days the chair was ritual, jus because she had a bad day. She would tell my daddy on the phone it was only for a couple of minutes, a senseless lie. I could always read lips. She was jealous of the attachment, I was daddy's little girl. I had realized forgive my debts as I forgive my debtors to let go of that angrier. .

Three: I almost got raped, changing my perception to men of the world

Four: I felt unloved, even though I was loved unconditionally.

The self pity created a high price prostitute. My first thought easy money from these horny men. Deborah-"as I looked in the crowd, towards the seat next to my son's wife, Gili.

"Deborah, a true friend, she would put in my purse all kinds of pamphlets and brochures of HIV, STD, alcohol abuse, drug abuse, self love and most important Why Jesus died for our sins. She never judged me her phrase for giving them to me was always, "she wanted me aware."

Taking my eyes off Deborah and back on the crowd, "Sober I thought of whom it was hurting, wives, daughters, sons, girlfriends, fiancées, finances, and homes! I didn't care when I was loaded, at least I'm not hurting.

Finally one day it hit me, I was hurting myself, I would always be to them the dirty secret, while abusing my body. This career had the wrong promises, of nothing coming later in life but misery. I was awkward, the outcast, the stranger in the store as they passed me with their wives and kids. My self esteem was gone, with the help of alcohol and drugs, my sins were being covered up."

"That lady in the mirror, I stared at myself to really see what I was becoming. Not a good picture not a good frame." "I had to stop now; I decided to do it cold turkey, tomorrow."

"I asked for help in this journey, from my D.O. She hypnotized me in her office, after I didn't respond, I was escorted out. She thought I was being a smart-alec, not even with book smarts she didn't know I was still sleep. She let go of my arm once I got in front of the chair in the waiting room. This consultation was over, but Chaim felt the real, very innocent and blessed." I glanced into space for a second.

"Grace was always there, using me as my own lesson, to an awakening of truth. In my deep sleep I would see my sins, pains and sorrows, in view and hearing in the unconscious world."

"My coma, produced a channel of a new wave of interception, in this stubborn sleep, rules could be different in apparel to the purpose of grand correction. My time for judgment of my righteousness within." "The monster had a strong hold on covering up the pain; my reflection only using me for capital gain to influence evil, my body was the weapon of choice."

"One of the helpers for truth using my own exaggeration to its fullest. A reverse of psychology, to the hidden truth. It starts once I begin to hate myself, and the hate gave redemption to get control and change, to a loveliness that would make me see the whole light. My sins were becoming the master of confusion. My soul says yes but my sins showing not right now. The time clock was ticking."

"The comforter gave warnings of danger zones in the style that would hit me deeper than my ears. I had to see I was worth a fight, the one and only Gershom, the love of self so I could love my neighbor. I was playing with my own mind, the comforter made sure I could see the truth. The steps were in my own wake up calling. I could hear in this level."

"My Daddy, staying with me praying and fasting, that a light would shine in my seeing, and/or my hearing. That was some of the things he said while I slept in my coma, the daddy of all daddy's." I turn toward my daughter and sent a blink to the man sitting next to her,

"My example, the sun-what an unselfish gift to all life, started to rise, the last day in rehabilitation. The clear words of a pray heard as my lids not yet open, "I pray come seek my daughter, save that which was lost"."

A slight cry heard from a female in the audience.

"The pray of a love for another well being, a humble prayer, Ira my god mother was praying for me."

"I want her to know it was answered."

A pause in my speech, chills filled my spine; I could hear soft echoes of choirs in harmony. The sound leaving as tender and quickly as it came.

Ira, smiling from ear to ear with tears running down her face, lifting her head up, "Thank you, thank you, thank you," rolled off her tongue, in a whisper.

"and many more, Thank you!" as I spoke softly.

A deep breath from the audience, Gershom couldn't hear.

My eyes now filling with tears, "Prayers are answered, filling my heart with bundles of joy, of this testimony."

"The servant and son of man, the begotten son, the son of GOD had my favor, authorizing many gifts to many soldiers, I am one."

I took a long breath into the microphone, "I speak amongst my own silence, in testimony to others, of my biography, the testimony. The surfacing of a new wave of saving souls, as me being a Real witness. The encouragement of a new change for the strongest love. My sleepwalking and seizures were taken away while in recovery at Saint John's, clean now 15years 2months 4days."

"Be enlightened with Love. GOD does Love us. GOD sent us a Savior that taught love and how to keep it, why question positive which equals a test will worth passing."

Spoken boldly and firm, and including sign language to the statement, "Jesus Christ, the Messiah, our Savior, Servant to man, Son of man, the only Begotten Son, The Son of GOD, I ask in those names and it shall be given, have mercy on Our souls, I ask, In GOD ""we"" trust!"

I begin to walk off the stage, as roses were thrown at my feet from the audience. Tears rolling down my face with a big smile, remember my mothers words, "the roses of flowers, have glory, in and of GOD."

Acknowledgment

To the highest that truly adores me, with nothing in return but LOVE. The love is so powerful that my father sends comforters to my aide with gifts that are abundant. The Protector, the Punisher, the Provider, these P's stand strong. The Doctor, the Forgiver, the Deliver, all the Power and the Glory in GOD.

In the name of Jesus Christ, our Savior, the servant and son to man, The begotten Son, the Son of GOD, Amen!!!

To a Queen that kept "me" within her prays with humbleness. The Beautiful mother, Temple Lee, you cracked the walls of darkness to a light of teachings even after your passing. Love for your only daughter, thank you for never stop praying for me, deep within Temple S.

To my Madame, for stepping in as my best friend after my mother's passing.

You and your husband gave me beautiful gifts every year, when mom pockets were less than pennies. Grandma Rose and Grandpa, thank you for helping a child, love being a child on Jesus Birthday. I do miss the both of you.

To other that are in the mist of all of the above, Matt Blosser, Demarcus, Polo, Stephanie Cole, Otis Pickett, Archie Jackson, Mrs. Elisse Brown, Soka, Grand Mccroy, yall passing coming in the last couple of years 2009 - 2012.

Evangeline "Lynn"(71-07), she's a motivation, she's Gershom in the friendship scenes with Derborah, a spiritual connection.

To the gifts given to me from above;

Neshia, a lilly in the valley, bright as the morning Sun. Let it shine, let it shine, let it shine. As your shine gets brighter and effects Jacob Lee (my only grand child), this seed is our blessing, my first born.

Keyat(Charles), you keep your root in the middle of a storm. Strength of GOD's plan is your motivation.

Rodney, the young man with a master plan, the Success of a warrior, the creation of a master piece from above.

Tee Tee, the go getter, his eye is on the sparrow and his leading you, fulfillment of his promise. Spread your wings claim your prize. Those pretty wings of Love

I'm glad my children, know and Love GOD!!!

My Big brother, Big Tra, we keep on keep it on, even though our trials are hard, we will always care. You have a hidden weapon against the world, Gizel, your wife, three words for her, sweet, strong, amazing. Julia(Matthew & Eric), your eyes always shows love. Lil Tre, giving it all you got, with a holy smile in the mist of confusion. Lil Temple, your name stands for itself. Olivia a soldier with a honest backbone. KevinLou, what a shy and out going twist to you, I can see the love.

To other big Brother, Kelvin the chief in command.

My other brothers:

Big Lou, I'm I my bro-sister keeper. YOU help me threw some very tough times, becoming a great friend from a sibling, Thank you with much Love

Garrett my son/ brother, so much joy, I'm glad I had a part of raising you.

Doug, the baby of the crew, love will conquer all

the love only siblings can have for each other, even in the test of times, Joy, Calvin, Pimala, and Issac

To my god children,

Mary, blessing you are to me, and a great blessing to Alani.

Lanesha, the sweetest thing I ever known.

Moet, so full of happiness that always shows

Markeda, oh how I love you

Cherelle(Cherish), rough rider with the pretty in pink

Demaruis, long time no hear, miss you

Rodnequa, my Ne Ne, my Ne Ne

Teachers.

Mr. D. the one whom saw my doors of opening and jump in at Brown Barge to show me. Mrs. Mccloud, one whom gave me uplifting.

Mrs. Magnum, the one who push me with a kiss on the cheek.

Andrew, the dream catcher of signs, highly favor.

NaNa(lil Jimmy, Miracle, Javon), this sister right here, we truly have a bond that can't be broken. Tell Robbie, he's the best brother in law a sista could have.

Tyesha, my sis, soul sister, GOD has plans for you.

Octavia(Lexus, Mercedes, & Cameron), my chick bad, my chick hood, my chick help me out when no one would

Re (Tylan Justin Janae, Tyler) this cousin here, crazy, sexy, cool

Tonya(Kreshaw, & Bria) always going to be my little cousin. So much love for you.

Debbie(Shawn), my lil sis, very wise beyond your time, very wise. Kiss them boyz for me, Aedenlove, Jerimiahjoy, Jashuea Sky and Harmon Star.

Shelly, chosen chosen chosen, my sista

Allyce, my friend of so many calibers.

John Moore, we talk we talk we talk, our opinions are the same, friend.

Darlene, you are a amazing lady with qualities of no compare. Giving birth to Tiffany, one the world greatest niece and Reefie keeping me with sooo many laughs.

Christy Crasty, boy our days as teenagers with Lynn(R.I.P.) was wild and very memorable, you're glowing with Light.

Sheila BFF, a person I confine in for exhaling, without the rumors of gossip, your smile lights up the room.

Stacey(the fantastic five), keep that smile and laughter, Lord knows some days for me it was will needed.

Takoshia, so positive in the mist of a storm

Amanda & Jason, where those crowns proudly.

Cousin Bev from Chi town, a true cousin to my mom, a true big cousin to me.

Byrd Tile family, special acknowledgment to Greg

Catoya & Bryan(Tory), a friendship that could never end

Paulette (Ray), indeed my aunt, indeed

Uncle Roosevelt, my great uncle, much respect.

Zack and Christian, the thoughtfulness of friendship towards others. To my Pickett's with love.

Josie, & Tiffany, my sista with a friendship that comes within.

Wanda, the full package in a small frame

Sarah, cousin you were the first to show support to my cause, five times

RTN(Raleigh Television Network), Ted(the teacher with a smile that brings on joyous cheer), Chasity (the one & only), Jason (helpful in every way you could), Carlos (oh my gosh thank you thank you thank you), Karyn(the pusher to do more,strong & positive), Ed (more like a uncle of caring) John (you actually sat thru my crazy life stories & listen) & Debbie(I sign my first production contract with you)

Brian Shorette, always love for the pure in spirit.

My god nephews,

Justin, Chris, aunt going to give you a spranking, smoochies

Brenda, years has pasted and we still can hold long conversations.

Rodney the first, we got four special gifts.

Michael Jackson, his music touching my emotion, especially when you're facing that man in the mirror.

Music losing two more Heavy D. motivation with a groove and Whitney Houston, vocals that can never be replaced.

To all the ladies and gentlemen that have lost their way in sin. The self esteem must come back to the abused, used, and belittled. Release, release, release, and be fulfilled, help is on its way!!!

To all the, I can't sleep at night, and GOD trying to tell me something, in readiness of writing this book.

GOD, THANK YOU, for everything I am, everything I was, everything I become to be.

THANK YOU, The ALPHA AND The OMEGA

To GOD special helpers in the introduction of Do you HEAR what I hear,

Chris Elliott, the concrete envoy of fine art, your illustration reached into my dream and brought it to sight.

Gizel Dumas, the jovial examiner, scanning and view gracefully, the herald of supportive improvement, correcting of vocabulary, the outline of helping a fellow Queen

The true meaning of why I wrote the book, this gift from GOD

Peccadillo, this word fits the whole explanation, coming to grips of Revelation.

Ye without sin cast the first stone. My reading of the Messiah answered many questions that were intriguing my mind. The reasoning for coming, to show and physically talk about our corrections of abomination basic around tradition and desolation of selfishness creating self destruction. The teachings revised in parables, of how to learn and become one with GOD the spirit. A physical sternness within our Savior, sunny as a visional insight, put in recordings for the common good for mankind.

So that leads me to baptismal. Baptism is the beginning chapter to start the launching of repentance of our sins, John the Baptize, baptized Jesus Christ, he whom without sin. The initiation to suffering for us, the trials came in a deeper way, tempting the true in spirit in his dream. Jesus to strong and knew what the destination was/is, the devil tried the good shepherd within sleep.

Dreams or a different caliber, nine times out of ten, we have no control over it, once we in. This was the way the tempter tried the servant to man, at the state we would fine a weakness, hungrier in your sleep, us the sinners; it would have been a mass of confusion. Which brings me back to baptismal, the son of man, to show us by suffering how temptation could not get to him, because the love of GOD is stronger, even in the mist of weakness, of what we think is the worst. The devil was trying to offer, the son of GOD the things of the world, food, shelter, and riches, for sinning, the answer and always will be "NO". The greatest fleshly teacher went threw all the steps of showing us he was a man in the flesh, by being here in the flesh.

The savior showed us by parables of understanding, miracles, and threw the Holy Spirit (our gut feeling, conscious), to jus begin to Love. The order to follow so you won't get lost a correction of offenses, crimes, indulgences, failing; wrong doing, and transgressions, our sins. The focus first Matthew: 22 37-40 get love for GOD with every piece of your soul, heart and mind. This light gives a way to a path of loving others as yourself, redemption.

Since our eyes are viewing openly, to peccadillo, so now our mind frame truly confused about loving our neighbor. The treatment of others is a big issue, why, the ways of the world is turning rotating in the fog of evil, finding more ways to conquer our souls (any kind of mental entertainment). I will elaborate more on the word; conquer, at the end of this hypothesis.

More answers to why to love, the enlightener, came to serve us with teachings. That wasn't all, could you imagine, someone constantly coming around you to find fault or bring you their problems with an emotional help me. Jesus passion for mankind was above and beyond. Saving and finding his lost sheep is the mission,

The begotten Son, crucifixion, showing how desolated the world is to innocent blood, the eye opener. His glorification of bearing the cross for us, this is no original love. The extreme power presented in the Resurrection of the Holy Spirit. This is what we should seek, the Holy Spirit.

Back to the theory which is the closure. Conquering, baptismal is repenting, and repenting is not sin free but the start of becoming sinless. To know you have sin!

My opinion, steps to conquering is having a plan, who, what, when, where, and how.

1. The who is you.
2. The what (I beg your pardon?), is conquering your soul.
3. The when, the time is now.
4. The where within your self.
5. The how is my synopsis, first move stop adding sin.

Using myself as the example, my past of how. I had a fighting angrier problem. I took notice that when I was drinking I became angry or lustful to a tasteless sense of no control. I would drink on the weekends at the club or chilling with friends. Stop the press, conquering, the club came with an opening to two sins that could come into effect.

The two sins, if indulge could possibly influencing the addition of doubling (angrier produces murders, a hate for thy neighbor and lust produces a jezebel). So I had to pump my brakes on that so I could conquer, relaxing from the clubs, help to start another process, observance to the obedience to the order.

My next step in this path was to begin subtracting my sins, gaining my self control. The staying at home help me to find myself loving my virtue while becoming closer to GOD, realizing it felt good to my individuality to love my Temple. I was controlling my angrier in a righteous mind and terms for lusting were getting dusted off my shoulder. I was seeing my worth, a Queen is Priceless.

My outlook and open opinion of repenting our sins is the beginning start of knowledge for a beautiful change. The sternness of not adding sins and to generate the process of deletion of temptation with all our soul and Faith in Christ, who die for our sins. My eyes are open, my ears hear, and my heart understands. The Mentor is he, life is the test, passing over is the grade, and the grade puts us in position within the everlasting Life.

A cheer to a greater world order of love, GOD is love. Jus believe!

Hebrew Meanings Of Names:

Benjamin- son of my right hand
Chaim- life
Deborah - honey bee
Gershom – a stranger there
Ira – watchful, descendant
Libbi – my heart
Molly - uncertain, maybe bitter
Razeil - GOD is my secret, or my mystery